KIMONO FOR
A CORPSE

By the same author:

The Wages of Zen
The Chrysanthemum Chain
A Sort of Samurai
The Ninth Netsuke
Sayonara, Sweet Amaryllis
Death of a Daimyo
The Death Ceremony
Go Gently, Gaijin

KIMONO FOR
A CORPSE

James Melville

St. Martin's Press
New York

Calligraphy by Mie Kimata

Library of Congress Cataloging-in-Publication Data

Melville, James.
      Kimono for a corpse / by James Melville.
        p.   cm.
   ISBN 0-312-01454-6 : $14.95
   I. Title.
PR6063.E439K5   1988
823'.914—dc19
                                              87-29940
                                                 CIP

First published in Great Britain by Martin Secken & Warburg Limited.

First U.S. Edition

10 9 8 7 6 5 4 3 2 1

This one is for Mark Schreiber –
scholar of crime fiction,
perceptive critic and good friend.

雪掃めの殺人事件

Chapter I

"Then there will be some individual foreign VIP visitors as usual, of course. Miss Hong Kong will be opening a new restaurant of that name in Kitano Ward on the twenty-fourth, and Professor Anatolii Pozdnyakov of the Soviet Academy of Sciences will give a public lecture at the City Library-Museum on the third of next month –"

"How do you spell that?" It was the twitchy young man from Kansai Television who wrote everything down.

"It's in the handout in front of you," the head of the Kobe City PR department said patiently, as he found it necessary to do several times every month at the briefing on forthcoming events of interest conducted for the benefit of the local media in a fair-sized conference room in the city hall, overlooking the broad boulevard which extends from the huge Sannomiya Station transport and underground shopping complex down past the New Port Hotel to the harbour. "Professor Pozdnyakov will be speaking about the information sent back by the probes landed on Venus in recent years. In Russian, with simultaneous interpretation. The Mayor will be in the chair."

"I'll bet he will," somebody muttered unkindly, probably the ultra-short-haired local correspondent for the Japanese edition of *Reader's Digest* who attended mostly for the sake of the coffee and particularly good cheesecake which was always handed round at the beginning. The Mayor's left-wing sympathies were well known.

Inspector Jiro Kimura of the Hyogo prefectural police force at last managed to catch the eye of Mie Nakazato, sitting a long way away at the other end of the big conference table. He was delighted to be rewarded with a wry little smile. Six months had passed since Mie had left her secretarial job at the headquarters of one of the tea ceremony schools in Kyoto and been taken on as a junior reporter for the women's page of the *Kobe Shimbun*, and her presence had made the last few Kobe City PR briefings much less boring than usual.

Kimura turned his head and gazed smugly out of the window. The wind was getting up quickly, visibly whipping the spiky fronds of the stubby palms which, along with some disciplined flower beds and patches of grass, testified to the municipality's concern for the environment and its determination to justify the English name "Flower Boulevard" which had been officially bestowed on the thoroughfare a good many years before. According to the weather report on the radio that morning Typhoon Penelope, which had been expected to take a course skirting the south-east of Japan, had veered north and was approaching the coast of the island of Shikoku; and as Kimura watched passers-by being buffeted about on the pavement below he thought the weathermen were right for once in warning that it might well lash straight across the island and the Inland Sea and pass over Kobe itself. That would mean a busy couple of days for the emergency services but was of only marginal personal concern to Kimura, whose own flat was in a solidly-built block most unlikely to lose its roof, well away from the steep hillsides

2

inland which were so vulnerable to landslides during the torrential rainstorms which accompany typhoons.

". . . and several delegations," the spokesman was saying as Kimura yawned and focused his attention on the proceedings again. He and the head of the traffic section usually represented Hyogo police on these occasions, although Kimura knew that the gnome like Inspector Imaizumi had his own lines of communication with City Hall, and a well-established drill for agreeing on the traffic control measures needed for big occasions like the annual Flower Festival. "We were delighted, for instance, to receive a letter from the Chairman of the Accrington and District Bonsai Group in England, and to learn that several of their leading members will be coming here to see the display in the park on Port Island next month during the course of their study tour of Japan. The Kobe Bonsai Federation is organising the show, but enthusiasts from all over the Kansai area will also be participating. Along with the chrysanthemum people, of course."

The PR man rambled on, looking anxiously at his watch from time to time, and Kimura began to wonder whether even the opportunity to rest his eyes on the delectable Mie really made it worth his while to sit through many more of these tedious meetings. As the head of the section responsible for keeping an eye on the sizeable expatriate community in the prefecture, he needed to know what was going on. On the other hand he had a great many alternative sources of information, and in any case Mie Nakazato had accepted his last two invitations to dinner even though she still lived with her parents in Kyoto and commuted to Kobe; over an hour's journey by train each way. Kimura seized every chance he could to urge on her the desirability of finding a place nearer to her office, and she was at last beginning to show signs of thinking seriously about it. As for the PR department's monthly briefings, there was no reason why one of his assistants shouldn't go on his behalf. Migishima perhaps: it would be a useful training exercise for him to be required to

3

sort out the wheat from the chaff when reporting back, as Kimura almost unconsciously did for his own chief, Superintendent Tetsuo Otani.

Kimura was still musing along these lines when the door was opened and a bespectacled young man hurried in, interrupted the spokesman in mid-sentence and whispered importantly to him before rushing out of the room again and leaving the door open. The PR man was obviously delighted, abruptly abandoning the subject of the forthcoming "Let's Help The Disabled!" campaign to which he had by then moved, and beaming round at the twenty or so people seated at the table.

"And now," he announced proudly but with an air of daring naughtiness, "it is my privilege to announce a surprise item . . . such a very newsworthy event indeed that we deliberately left it off today's agenda. A *special* information pack will be distributed shortly. And here in person to tell us about it is none other than —" he cocked an ear and was seemingly reassured by the sound of voices in the corridor outside, " – none other than Madame Masako Yasuda!"

Kimura turned and stared towards the open door with just as lively an interest as most of the other people in the room as the famous lady swept in, followed by an entourage of at least half a dozen people including the young man who had warned the spokesman of her imminent arrival. The doyenne of high fashion in Japan was wearing what he presumed was one of her own creations, a severely cut black suit with padded shoulders and pencil-slim skirt which set off the dramatic pallor of her face and did little to soften the hauteur of her expression, which was probably in any case justified by the size of the diamond brooch at her breast and the matching earrings revealed by her forties-style permanent wave.

Masako Yasuda had to be pushing fifty at least, Kimura reflected as she passed near him, but she looked a little less and certainly smelt good. He had no idea what the perfume was: it was none of the four or five leading French brands he could identify, and it conflicted intriguingly with the almost

4

funereal effect produced by her clothes, her plain court shoes and her skinny legs in seamed black stockings. Arriving at the head of the table, Madame Yasuda acknowledged with a distant, almost pained smile the scattered applause which greeted her appearance. Then, queenly and remote, she sank gracefully into the chair held for her by the awed PR man and gazed at a large aerial photograph of Kobe Harbour on the wall opposite her as he launched himself into an incoherently fervent speech of welcome.

When he eventually subsided it was not the guest of honour who responded, but a man who introduced himself as Hiroshi Uehara, and to whom Kimura took an instant dislike. He disliked Uehara's expensive haircut and his Chester Barrie suit of finest blue-grey mohair. He loathed his Armani silk shirt and the maddening subtlety of the Sulka tie which set it off so effectively. Above all, he hated the fact that this Uehara person was extraordinarily good-looking and at least ten years younger than himself. Kimura was in fact so thoroughly put out that he failed to observe the slightly dazed expression on Mie Nakazato's face and the tip of her tongue moistening her lips as she hung upon the newcomer's words; and this was just as well.

Uehara, it emerged, was Madame Yasuda's business manager, and it was he who, in a pleasantly caressing baritone speaking voice and with the skills of an experienced actor, announced that "Mode International" would take place over a period of several days early in November. Top designers from the United States, Paris and London had accepted invitations to participate, and would be bringing their own favourite models to show off their latest creations in a show designed and choreographed by New York's own Sherry Rose. The ladies and gentlemen of the media had heard, Uehara assured his audience with comradely confidence, of the highly successful "Best Six" shows staged from time to time by the Hanae Mori organisation in Tokyo. He could assure them that "Mode International" was conceived on an altogether more ambitious scale and that during the exciting

5

November days to come Kobe would be the focus of interest of the entire world of fashion, whose most prominent editors and writers would be descending upon the city from every continent to cover the event.

At this point Uehara made an almost imperceptible gesture towards the back of the room, and two girls in trim shocking-pink skirts and waistcoats over long sleeved polka-dot blouses and wearing white gloves and little hats tripped forward bearing piles of bulky olive-green folders which they distributed to the people round the table, one taking each side. "Inside your information pack you will find full details of the event," Uehara continued. "Photographs and biodata for all the participating designers and their top models. Everything else that we have been able to think of, and believe me, Madame Yasuda here makes sure we think of everything." Uehara made a deferential little bow in the direction of his employer, who smiled faintly in response and then flashed a film-star grin round the room. Kimura found it utterly nauseating.

"The shows will take place at your magnificent 'Tamahimeden' wedding hall, quite the most spacious and beautiful of its kind we've seen anywhere in the country. And as of today a 'Mode International' administration and information office is being set up right there on the spot, under the temporary direction of Mr Kinjo here until I can myself come down from Tokyo to be at your service from the week before the gala opening ceremony." He indicated Mr Kinjo, a much older man who looked positively seedy compared with Uehara, and Kinjo half stood, hung his head and muttered something incomprehensible.

"As Mr Kinjo says, it will be his pleasure and mine to cooperate with you and with your media colleagues from all over the world in every way. What about a special slogan, Mr Chairman? Shall it be 'Kobe à la Mode'? Well, whatever you decide, on behalf of Madame Yasuda and all of us, I thank you for your courtesy in being here today."

Then it was suddenly all over. The PR man's "heartfelt,

6

sincere" thanks were hurriedly truncated when Masako Yasuda floated out of the room, attended by her courtiers and still not having uttered a word, and he had to pursue her in order to see her off the premises with due ceremony. Mie Nakazato had been sitting near the door and she too slipped out before Kimura could waylay her.

Thwarted, Kimura rose to his feet and went to peer moodily out of the window just as the designer emerged from the main entrance below and was ushered into a glossy Lincoln limousine which had been drawn up as closely as possible to the building so as to minimise her exposure to the blustering winds. Uehara did not appear to be with Madame Yasuda and Kimura was further vexed not to be able to confirm his one encouraging suspicion about the man, which was that he might have a bald spot on the top of his well-groomed head. With this thought in mind, he was the more startled when, feeling a hand on his arm, he turned to realise not only that the man had not even left the now almost empty room, but that he was indeed standing at his side.

Uehara's manner when he spoke this time was businesslike and straightforward. "Inspector Kimura? My apologies for disturbing you. I wonder if we might have a word? Madame Yasuda asked me to apologise for not being able to stay herself. She has an urgent appointment elsewhere in town."

Kimura was not only flattered to be sought out, but also much cheered by the fact that he could now see clearly that Hiroshi Uehara was distinctly thin on top. Furthermore, the cologne he used was one which he himself had lately abandoned after Mie had hinted that she found its fragrance slightly cloying. "My pleasure," he said with a return to something approaching his normal affability. "Nice to meet you."

"I was told by the PR people here that a senior man from the Hyogo police headquarters usually came along to their monthly briefings, and had our chairman point you out." Uehara threw a brief, practised smile in the direction of the chairman, who had returned from his duties below and was hovering obsequiously nearby. The official gobbled it up gratefully, a performing seal rewarded for his efforts. "Look, I have to get myself unstuck from these people," Uehara then murmured conspiratorially to Kimura, "then I'm going straight over to the Tamahimeden. Would you by any chance have time to join me in the car and have a cup of coffee with me there? There's something I think you people ought to know."

Kimura agreed at once, and had been waiting and glancing through the contents of his information pack for no more than two or three minutes in the downstairs lobby when Uehara was escorted down by what looked like the entire personnel of the publicity department and was finally able to liberate himself from them. A rather less grand but nevertheless satisfactorily sleek hire car was now in position outside, the driver braced against the gusts of wind, holding his uniform cap in place with one hand as he stood poised to open the door for them with the other.

"Let's hope there won't be any more typhoons coming our way after this one," Uehara remarked when they were safely enclosed. "Though I suppose there's still a chance right through to the end of November. I suppose you know the Tamahimeden pretty well, Inspector?"

Kimura never enjoyed admitting ignorance, but on this occasion could do no more than fudge. "Well, I know of it, of course. But as a matter of fact I haven't had occasion to go inside as yet."

"It's weird. Like something out of Disneyland. God knows what the *gaijin* designers and models will make of it, or the journalists. But the punters will love it." Kimura was warming rapidly to Uehara, and entirely approved of his evident assumption that the two of them were birds of a feather, wordly-wise cynics who observed with tolerant humour the antics of the hoi polloi.

The Tamahimeden Wedding Hall is located no more than a few blocks away from Kobe City Hall, close to the Trade Centre and the Kaigan Hospital near the waterfront to the east of the modern harbour and container terminals, and they were soon approaching it. Although he must have passed the

8

place many times in the couple of years since it had been built, Kimura had never given it more than a passing look. Now, as the car swept through the outer gates and up to the main entrance, he considered it objectively.

The overwhelming impression the Kobe Tamahimeden gives is one of almost indecently luxurious spaciousness, occupying as it does a colossal area of prime building land approaching an acre in extent; and this in a city, like almost every other in Japan, where space is at such a premium that strangely-shaped, improbably tiny buildings are everywhere squeezed into odd corners and a garden is often contrived in two square metres. The wedding hall boasts a façade of narrow, lofty white arches forming a kind of outer cloister. Behind are slender gothic-style windows, with stained-glass panels above the elevated main entrance approached by a gracious flight of steps each side, and a fountain supported by a trio of bronze cherubs in a vaguely Grecian alcove below. From a distance the building looks vaguely like an expensive mosque in some arriviste oil sheikhdom, sited oddly in the middle of a golf course, for it is surrounded by carefully groomed grassy knolls and hillocks. "Makes you think, doesn't it?" Kimura offered as the automatic glass doors slid open before them. "Youngsters who are going to spend the rest of their lives living in a one-room apartment will lay out a fortune on their wedding day just to be able to remember the couple of hours they had the run of a palace."

Once inside Kimura saw at once how apt Uehara's remark about Disneyland had been. The lobby was vast but remorselessly cute, like a royal ballroom in a children's cartoon film. Chandeliers twinkled high above their heads, while the decor featured great swathes of pink and burgundy velvet. To one side was a curious white vehicle, which looked to Kimura a little like Cinderella's magic coach. Then he thought again and remembered a happy summer afternoon in the south of France during his European year as a student of modern languages. A flower festival, a float bearing a bevy of waving girls in bikinis, a smile intercepted, a kiss blown in his direction and honoured that evening, when wine had helped

9

to make his French seem less halting. Yes, the flimsy contraption was more like that processional float . . .

"Wedding photos to end all wedding photos," Uehara suggested, leading the way across the lobby and raising a hand in affable acknowledgement of the profound bow with which they were greeted by a man in a black coat and striped trousers who had appeared from behind a screen to one side. "They tell me you aren't married, Inspector."

"No, I'm not." Kimura's response was curtly off-putting. He resented the thought that Uehara had been making enquiries about him, and the implication that the man-to-man approach had been adopted quite deliberately as a means of flattering and disarming him. "Look," he said as Uehara opened the door of a small office in a short corridor off the main lobby. There was a card on the outside bearing the name "Mode International" in elegant roman script, while the room itself was furnished in neutrally good taste and had an unused look about it. "Look, I have to get back to head-quarters pretty soon. If you'd just let me know what's on your mind . . ."

Uehara was all diplomatic concern. "I'm so sorry, Inspector. You're a very busy man, and I've been rambling on. Forgive me. Won't you just take a seat for five minutes? I'll keep to the point, I promise you." He depressed a switch on the telephone console on the desk. "Coffee for two. Right away," he said peremptorily, and released the switch without waiting for an answer. Then he sat down himself and looked directly at Kimura for almost the first time since he had first approached him in the conference room at the City Hall. In view of Uehara's earlier expansive manner Kimura was more than a little surprised to see something uncommonly like deep anxiety in his face.

"I sought you out very deliberately, Inspector," he said. "You have a considerable reputation in this city, as the most sophisticated, switched-on senior man at police head-quarters. It's like this . . . We have a very serious problem on our hands."

10

Chapter II

Superintendent Tetsuo Otani settled himself in his usual chair and contemplated his two principal lieutenants. The approach of a typhoon must always be a matter for concern to him, because his responsibilities covered a huge area embracing not only Kobe itself and the several other sizeable cities and towns in Hyogo prefecture, but also remote countryside in which there are villages in almost every valley, all vulnerable to landslides from the precipitous hills looming over them. His men, as well as those of the fire and ambulance services, were in for a busy night, for a typhoon rarely struck the main islands of Japan directly without causing widespread damage, injuries and loss of life.

Nevertheless, though very much on the alert, Otani was basically in a good mood. There was after all an emergency of some sort or another every day of the year, and more people were killed every week in routine road accidents in his bailiwick than even the most destructive typhoon could be expected to account for. It did not do to become twitchy, and

11

on the whole all was right with his world. The lunch served that day at the regular weekly meeting of the Kobe South Rotary Club, of which he was a proud if unreliable member, had consisted for a change of a very acceptable grilled salmon steak with mixed vegetables, followed by the ever popular *puriin* or baked custard instead of ice cream, a regular alternative which he abominated. Furthermore, his wife Hanae had in the middle of the morning made one of her rare telephone calls to him at the office to tell him excitedly that their daughter Akiko had written from England to report that her husband had been recalled to the Osaka head office of the trading company for which he worked after five highly successful years in London, and it seemed that further promotion was in the air. So he and Hanae could look forward to seeing plenty of their small grandson, who could go to a good kindergarten and hope thereafter to stay on the crucially important Japanese educational escalator which, in the fullness of time, should deposit him in the right university.

"Thank you both for coming early as usual. We have forty-five minutes before the others join us, and obviously the typhoon will be the main item on the agenda this week. I imagine you both know it's expected to pass over just west of the city during the course of this evening. It must be two or three years since one came this close."

Kimura looked up from the olive-green folder he was nursing on his knees and nodded. "Yes. September, three years ago. And they've gouged out a tremendous amount of hillside to make Rokko Island since then. It could be quite dangerous on the other side of town if there's a lot of rain. The excavations aren't too near your house, are they, Chief?"

"Rather too near for comfort," Otani said. "But I expect we'll be all right. We always have been in the past. All the same, I'll be at home by the phone in case I'm needed rather than down here in the duty room tonight."

Inspector "Ninja" Noguchi didn't bother to comment. His views on the massive civil engineering projects which had literally transformed the map of Kobe and the hills to its

12

north-east since the mid-seventies, and created whole new districts on the man-made Port and Rokko Islands, were even more reactionary than Otani's own and were well known. He merely sniffed, noisily ran his tongue round his remaining teeth and hunched even lower in his chair.

"Anyway, more of that later, no doubt," Otani continued. "What else do we need to talk about? Have you got anything for us, Kimura-kun?"

Kimura looked at his watch, which he had prudently checked against the digital wall-clock in the duty room on his way up to Otani's office. He had recently read an article somewhere about personal electrical fields and concluded that his endless trouble with watches was not just a matter of bad luck but of his own magnetic power, which had cheered him up. He would have preferred to talk to his superior at some length about his conversation with Uehara rather than having to report hurriedly before the weekly heads of section meeting began, but could at least summarise it and get a preliminary reaction in ten or fifteen minutes.

"There is something, yes. I was over at the city hall this morning for their monthly briefing meeting."

"Ah, yes. The usual stuff, I suppose."

"Most of it, yes. Some Russian scientist coming to give a lecture, some bonsai enthusiasts from England –"

"Really? *Bonsai*, you said? Whereabouts in England?"

Otani was all eager attention, and Kimura sighed inwardly as he tried to remember. "I'm sorry, I really can't recall, and I didn't bring the handout with me. Somewhere I've never heard of, anyway. I'll check and let you know, if you're really interested. The big thing, though –"

"I am, actually," Otani said, glancing modestly down at a particularly worn spot on the old brown lino which had needed replacing since long before he took over command of the Hyogo force. "The fact is, I've recently been made President of the Rokko Bonsai Club."

Even Noguchi was taken aback to the extent of opening his eyes. "*You?* Since when have you been a bonsai expert?"

13

Otani gave him a shy little smile. "Oh, I'm not. Not in the least. My father was, years ago. And of course he left me all his and I try to keep them going. You know, re-potting and trimming the roots every two or three years, tidying up the foliage about this time of the year, a sprinkle of lime during the winter, just routine. I've never attempted to grow any new ones. I suppose it was my juniper that attracted a certain amount of attention when my wife persuaded me to show a few at the local display a few years ago. It is rather nice. Nearly a hundred years old."

"And now you're the President. Well, well." It was impossible to tell from Noguchi's battered, expressionless features whether he was impressed or amused by the news of Otani's elevation and his unexpected parade of ultra-small-scale silvicultural expertise.

Otani himself had his suspicions but decided to disregard them. "So I'd be glad if you'd let me have the details, Kimura."

"Yes, yes, of course. Right after the meeting," Kimura promised hurriedly. "But if I could just quickly pass on to this other matter —"

Otani made an open-handed gesture of invitation. "Please. My fault for interrupting you."

Kimura closed his eyes momentarily to rearrange his thoughts, and then indicated the folder in his lap before launching into a reasonably concise account of the irruption of Masako Yasuda and her retinue into the normally dreary proceedings of the monthly meeting at the city hall, the speech by Hiroshi Uehara and Uehara's request for a private chat at the Tamahimeden.

Noguchi appeared to pay no attention, but Otani listened politely for some time before becoming impatient. "Yes, yes. I'm sure this will be a very big affair, Kimura. I dare say my wife will want to go. And I'm glad you're obviously well briefed about the details, but time's getting on, and . . ." His voice trailed off in mid-sentence, and Kimura hastened as he read the warning signs.

14

"I'm sorry, sir," he said with an air of brisk efficiency. "I was about to come to the point, which is that Uehara told me that the Yasuda fashion house in Tokyo has within the past week or two received a series of cleverly staged extortion demands, from some anonymous individual or group in this area, threatening to wreck the project unless the Yasuda people pay protection money."

"How much?" Noguchi spoke so rarely at their three-way conferences that his interventions invariably stopped whichever of the others was speaking in his tracks.

Kimura shook his head irritably as though troubled by a fly. "Two hundred thousand US dollars. But there's no indication of how this extortioner proposes to 'wreck' the show, as he apparently puts it. If they don't pay."

"What do you mean by 'cleverly staged' extortion demands? Something unusual about the technique?" Otani was looking less bored.

"No, Chief, I meant they moved through various stages. Escalating, as it were, or more accurately, becoming more menacing. The first was a phone call Uehara hardly thought about: somebody rang his office and left a message with his secretary to say that the caller hoped the Mode International show in Kobe would be a great success. A bit peculiar, but nothing more. A few days later a woman caller rang with another message, to the effect that she hoped nothing would happen at the show to upset any of the visiting designers. Then last week –"

"These visiting designers. Who are they?"

Long experience had taught Kimura to expect interruptions whenever he embarked on an attempt at a connected explanation of a situation, and he manfully suppressed his exasperation as he opened the folder and pulled out a set of photographs. "From England, Wesley Wilberforce. Here he is."

Otani studied the glossy photograph of a middle-aged man wearing no-nonsense glasses and a conventional dark suit. His expression seemed to be one of slight disapproval, and

15

the only hint of his involvement in anything as creative as fashion was the slight fullness of the silver hair where it was brushed back over the ears. "He looks rather like a business man to me," Otani observed as he passed the picture to Noguchi, who took it with an air of some surprise.

"That's what he is," Kimura said. "He's very highly thought of by the British aristocracy, I believe. He's made clothes for duchesses, it says here, and the wives of leading racehorse owners. The notes say that he'll be accompanied by his associate Terry Phipps, and his favourite model Vanessa Radley."

"Kept her photo for yourself, have you?" Noguchi never lost an opportunity to get at Kimura over his indefatigable womanising, but Kimura sniffed loftily and produced photographs of both Phipps and the model. Vanessa Radley was blonde and looked both haughty and pained, while for his picture Phipps was wearing a frilled shirt open almost to the waist, a heavy gold pendant and a boyish grin. Since he was clearly well into his fifties, like Wesley Wilberforce, the effect was unpleasing.

Kimura selected another picture and handed it over. "This is Jean-Claud Villon, from Paris."

A darkly handsome man of forty or so with lined features and a sardonic lift to one eyebrow looked wearily up at Otani, who studied the likeness for a few seconds and then favoured Kimura with one of his rare smiles. "He looks a bit like you, Kimura-kun. Dresses almost as well, too."

"Why, thank you, Chief! I'm really flattered," Kimura said with a shock of pure pleasure.

"Really? Oh. Well, who's next?"

There was a perceptible pause before Kimura continued. "Villon isn't bringing anyone with him. America is represented by Marian Norton, whose particular model is a black girl called Barbi Mingus. This is what they look like."

Although he always professed to believe that all Westerners looked alike and that he found them quite inscrutable, Otani reflected as he looked at the glossy

16

photographs of Marian Norton's lined, chalk-white face and the severe cut of her straight hair, that here was a complex, intense woman, who could be anything between forty and sixty. Her model, Barbi Mingus, looked nobly menacing. Her great eyes were half closed, and her lips were firmly set. Her hair had been shaved high on either side of her head and rose up short and straight on the top which had been trimmed to a perfect horizontal plane, as though with the aid of a set-square. The black woman's elegant neck was so proudly arched as to make her appear almost like a piece of sculpture. "Interesting pair," was all Otani said as he laid the pictures down on the low table between them.

"I don't know whether this one counts as a visitor or not," Kimura said. "It's Tsutomu Kubota." Before he could pass the photograph to Otani it was plucked from his hand by Noguchi, who could move fast on the rare occasions he chose to do so, and who now peered closely at it as Kimura manfully tried to carry on. Otani was still looking down at the pictures of the two Americans and either did not notice Noguchi's action or chose to appear not to do so.

"Kubota made his name in Europe, of course, not here. His main salon is in Paris, but three years ago he opened branches in New York and London. And it says he has homes in all three cities. But he was born here in Kobe, so the Mode International show will be a homecoming for him."

Otani looked up at last. "What did you say? Born here?"

"Yes. About thirty-six years ago, must have been." Both Otani and Kimura looked in surprise at Noguchi, who stared unseeingly at the wall for a few seconds, then sighed noisily and tossed the picture on top of the others. "Only he wasn't called Tsutomu Kubota then."

"You mean you *know* him, Ninja?" Kimura was incredulous and obscurely offended. Otani said nothing, merely glancing from one to the other of them as he bent forward and picked up the print himself.

After being made to look at so many pictures of more or less outlandish-looking foreigners, it came as something of a

17

relief to him to see the likeness of a perfectly ordinary Japanese. True, most studio photographs of Japanese depict them in formal old-fashioned poses and make them look acutely uncomfortable, whereas Kubota was obviously entirely at ease. There was something else about his expression, too, which Otani had noticed before in the faces of Japanese who had lived for some years outside their native country and which his own daughter Akiko and her husband had already been developing when he and Hanae had seen them in London.

It wasn't exactly a matter of confidence, for they had always had plenty of that. It was more an air of humorous nonchalance, an absence of that earnest, dedicated role-consciousness which seemed to afflict most of the people Otani encountered, whether they were the company presidents and professional men who frequented Rotary or, at the other end of the scale, waitresses, ticket-collectors or rank-and-file gangsters. He was perfectly well aware that he displayed a careful public face himself towards all but his closest relatives and the handful of trusted associates headed by Noguchi and Kimura: the only people in the world he really cared about, outside his immediate family. Kubota, or whatever his real name was, had that liberated look that was so hard to define, and Otani allowed his gaze to flicker briefly from the image on the glossy paper to the familiar, battered features of his old friend Noguchi. After the traumatic experience of discovering some years earlier that Noguchi had fathered a son by a Korean common-law wife, it would not surprise him if another of his by-blows were to turn up out of the blue. "Well, Ninja?" he enquired gently.

"Well what?"

"Kimura-kun was asking if you knew him. Obviously you do. What can you tell us about him?"

Whatever might be passing through Noguchi's mind, he seemed to Otani to be if anything slightly amused rather than embarrassed or emotionally affected. "Nothing much," he rumbled after an apparent pause for recollection. "Real

18

name's Ezaki. Right young tearaway he was twenty years ago. Still at high school, father a bus driver. Brilliant artist, lightning sketches. Worked out a nice little number calling at well-off women's houses in the afternoon. Portrait sketch for a thousand yen."

"Nothing very terrible about that, Ninja," Kimura objected.

Noguchi ignored him and continued, "Personable kid at sixteen, looked two or three years older. Anyway, there was at least one woman, rich doctor's wife, bored to tears probably. Fancied him, very likely led him on, posed for him in the nude. Kept the sketches, of course, but young Ezaki did some more from memory and tried a spot of blackmail on her. Unmistakable background, see, and this woman has a little scar on her belly. Silly kid. She told him to come back next day, laughed her head off when he'd gone and gave us a ring. I was assistant DI in Nada Ward then. Kept the appointment and gave him a bit of a talking to." Noguchi's lips twisted briefly in what might have been a smile. "Ezaki must have given her a good time. Anyway, she didn't bear malice. Nice woman. Had a sister, head of an art college in Nagoya. Fixed up for Ezaki to go there when he got out of high school. Did well, got a job afterwards with Hanae Mori then started on his own and called himself Kubota."

As Noguchi sank back into the depths of his chair, exhausted by his long speech, Kimura glared at him. "How come you know so much about what happened after a trivial case of juvenile delinquency like that?" he demanded.

"Kept in touch with the lady, didn't I?" Noguchi's eyes remained firmly closed as he responded, and Otani winked at Kimura, who shrugged and forced a disbelieving smile.

"Yes, well, all very interesting," Otani said then. "So these are the visiting designers and the foreign models. And you've already told us about Masako Yasuda of course. All right. Now you really must get back to this business of the threats. The others will be here in a few minutes." Kimura goggled at him, outraged by Otani's bland implication that he was to blame for the lengthy digression. "Well? You were saying that Uehara's secretary took these two disconcerting phone messages. Then something else happened last week. What was that?"

Kimura breathed in deeply, and tried again. "Last week a letter arrived, addressed to Masako Yasuda, postmarked here in Kobe. Anonymous, of course. It offered 'insurance cover' for the show in return for a single 'premium'. The two hundred thousand US dollars I mentioned, payable to a numbered account in Switzerland. If the money isn't transferred by ten days before the show opens, there will be 'accidents', it said."

"I see. And did Uehara show you this letter?"

"No."

"We ought to have a look at it. Presumably he's reported all this to the Tokyo police? I'm surprised they haven't been in touch."

"They haven't reported it. Uehara said he wanted our local advice on what to do."

Otani shrugged. "Well, he can hardly expect us to suggest they should pay up, can he? What did you tell him?"

"I said it sounded like a try-on and that my top-of-the-head reaction was to advise them to ignore it or take it up with the Met in Tokyo, as you mentioned. Beyond that all I could say was that we'd take delivery of the information and consider our position."

"Yes. I'd probably have reacted the same way. Well, look into it carefully, Kimura, and we'll have another talk in a day or two. Heaven forbid that it should be another joker trying something along the lines of the Glico and Morinaga confectionery affairs. Or the same people."

Otani looked from one to the other of his colleagues, his face grim. Most of the blame for the bungling incompetence of the police in dealing with the mysterious "Man With 21 Faces" who had made fools of them and terrified the general public a year or two previously had rested with their colleagues in neighbouring Osaka, but their own morale had been severely shaken by the affair.

20

"Jokers don't have numbered accounts in Switzerland," Noguchi growled reassuringly as a tap on the door heralded the arrival of the heads of the other sections for their weekly meeting with their commander, but even he didn't sound altogether convinced. Kimura suppressed a shudder at the thought of the jeering letters the newspapers had received from the still elusive person or persons who had successfully kidnapped the president of one of Japan's biggest confectionery manufacturing companies and threatened to poison its products and those of their chief rival. Momentarily he saw himself and his chief the butts of similar ridicule in the pages of the national press, and avoiding the ignorant questions of television reporters encamped outside the main entrance of their own headquarters building.

"Well, let's hope you're right, Ninja," Otani said as they all rose and began to move over to the large conference table at the other side of his office. "There's no sense in getting excited at this stage, anyway. Oh, Kimura-kun. Don't forget to let me know about the bonsai experts from England, will you? Come in, gentlemen! Good afternoon. Well, we're in for a wet and windy twenty-four hours, it seems . . ."

Chapter III

"So I thought I'd probably better not mention to Kimura that I already knew about this fashion show. You know how he hates to be upstaged." Hanae tried not to smile as she took the empty bowl her husband was holding out to her and refilled it from the lacquer rice container which reposed by her side on the tatami matting along with their newly-acquired electric gadget for keeping a spare flask of *sake* warm. There was still a little of the chicken and some Chinese noodles left in the dish on the low table at which they were seated with their legs dangling into the *kotatsu* pit at the bottom of which a low-powered heater would be placed when the evenings turned really chilly. The dish was also heated by electricity, and Otani sometimes complained that the various leads trailing across the floor from the wall-socket in their all-purpose living-room at mealtimes made it look like a television studio.

"Anyway, this fellow Watanabe only mentioned it in passing. The main theme of his talk was this campaign of the

Prime Minister's to make us all buy a hundred dollars' worth of foreign goods. It's hardly surprising that Watanabe's all for it – what was that?"

By the time Otani had arrived home the worst onslaught of the typhoon was imminent and Hanae had already slid the stout wooden storm shutters from their box-like housings outside the windows of the old house and bolted them into place. Their rattling as the savage gusts of wind and the driving rain searched for entry had accompanied both their evening bath and the meal which followed. The new sound which had disturbed Otani was a distant hollow booming which became intermittent until a rending screech was followed by a decisive crash and the sound of breaking glass.

Hanae cocked an ear. "It was up the hill. It sounds as if the illuminated sign outside the new apartment terraces has blown down."

"Ah, very likely," Otani agreed with an air of lazy satisfaction. " 'Rokko Park Royal Heights' indeed! If ever there was a case for a landslide, it's that monstrosity . . . oh, very well, I'm sorry. You know I didn't mean it."

Hanae was loath to wish ill upon anyone, and was easily distressed by even mock ruthlessness. Resolutely she reverted to the previous subject. "If this Mr Watanabe is such a bad character I'm surprised that he was invited to speak at your club in the first place."

Otani smiled at her with much tenderness. "Ha-chan. If we only had respectable citizens to talk at our meetings the Programme Committee of the Rotary Club of Kobe South would soon run out of candidates. Yutaka Watanabe was a considerable catch. President of Wakamatsu department store chain, no less. And the fact that we've been reading in the papers for several months that the other board members are trying to get rid of him made him an even bigger attraction. We had an exceptional turn-out today in spite of the weather, I can tell you."

"I'm surprised that he mentioned Masako Yasuda's fashion show, all the same. The magazines have been

23

gossiping about her being his mistress for years, but. . . "

Otani's swarthy face was illuminated by a brief grin. "Business associate, please. That's one of the main reasons for the trouble with the Wakamatsu board of directors, I gather. They aren't too worried about the bills for the building works and fancy furniture at his own house and the homes of his other two mistresses being paid by the company. Or the school and college fees for their various children by Watanabe. People are quite tolerant about that sort of thing. Colourful old rogue, they say to themselves. They still tend to feel that way about Tanaka, after all. What's the good of clawing your way up from nothing to become prime minister if you don't grab a handful of fruit for yourself? No, if Masako Yasuda were simply one of the mistresses everything would be fine. It's the 'Boutique Masako' in every Wakamatsu store in the country that bothers them."

"But why ever should it? They always seem to be doing good business whenever I go into the Wakamatsu in either Osaka or Kobe. You know, I think the wind seems to be dying down just a little, don't you?"

"Yes, I think you're right. Maybe it's passing. Or else we could be in the eye of the typhoon, in which case it'll pick up again in a while." Otani picked his teeth thoughtfully and drank some green tea before answering Hanae's first question. "That's just the point. 'Madame Yasuda', as Kimura tells me she likes to be called, is making a fortune out of those boutiques, but the Wakamatsu shareholders aren't. Apart from her own clothes she sells all sorts of lines which compete directly with the main store. Making huge profits the Wakamatsu directors think should figure in the company's balance sheet, not hers. Watanabe gave her the boutique concession in the flagship store in Tokyo about ten years ago, you see, for some ridiculously small annual rental. A thank-you present for his lady friend when he decided she was getting a bit old for the mistress role. Rather like the way ex-geisha are often set up as mama-sans in bars when they retire."

24

Hanae was intrigued enough to refill their sake cups from the spare flask and drink from her own without even noticing. "How on earth do you know all this?"

Otani shrugged his shoulders casually. "I dare say the magazines have it by now, but I remember the Baron telling me years ago, well before he. . . died. He knew everything like that." They both fell silent for a while, remembering the suicide of their old patron and friend, and Hanae fumbled briefly for her husband's hand.

"Yes," Otani went on after a while, gently disengaging himself. "He used to rather enjoy passing on the scandal he picked up while he was President of the Chamber of Commerce. Anyway, it seems that Madame recognised a good thing when she saw one, and interpreted her agreement with Wakamatsu as entitling her to open similar boutiques on the same terms in any provincial branch she cared to. And Watanabe carried enough weight with the other directors to let her get away with it. Six months ago, and without consulting them, he signed a renewal of her agreement for a further five years without any upward revision. The board members were furious, and as you know from the papers he miscalculated the strength of the opposition to him, and the damage done by rumours that a hefty percentage of Masako Yasuda's profits go straight into his personal bank accounts. Hence Watanabe's present posture as the responsible Japanese businessman worried about his country's reputation in the west. The Wakamatsu stores have always specialised in expensive imported goods, of course, so he can boost sales and encourage his few remaining cronies on the board to go on toeing his line as well as pleasing his foreign suppliers."

Hanae shook her head. "It all sounds too complicated for me," she said. "And I don't think I'm really very interested. . . except that he doesn't seem to be particularly discreet about his relationship with Masako Yasuda."

"No. Quite the reverse. On the contrary, when he mentioned her today in the course of his speech it was as 'my internationally famous associate' who was unselfishly doing

25

her bit too by bringing these gaijin designers to Japan and encouraging sales of their clothes here. So you'd better economise on the housekeeping for a few weeks and treat yourself to a French dress."

Hanae decided not to burden her husband with enlightenment on the subject of *haute couture* prices. The fury of the typhoon outside definitely did seem to be abating, and there had been no telephone call from headquarters to report any serious emergencies. It was pleasant sitting there behind the sturdy wooden defences which had protected them both for so many years, and Otani himself since his infancy, and Hanae was minded to make the most of it. "Tell me more about the bonsai people from England," she suggested.

"Ah, yes. I haven't been able to find out a lot. They're coming from a city called Accrington. It's in Lancashire Prefecture in the north, Kimura got Migishima to look it up in some sort of guide-book they have in their section. He couldn't find anything in the book about the bonsai society, but apparently the municipality has, or used to have, a famous football team called Accrington Stanley. Or perhaps Stanley is the name of the captain of the team. Migishima couldn't quite work it out, but was insistent that Stanley is a man's name. It does seem a bit odd to me to think of English people growing bonsai. I shall be quite interested to meet them if I can be at the regional display when they go there."

"It seems there's quite a vogue for bonsai all over the world these days," Hanae put in pensively. "A few weeks ago when I went to my Western-style cookery class at the YWCA in Kobe there was an Indian lady there. Visiting from Bombay. Mrs Prakash brought her."

"And who might Mrs Prakash be?"

"Oh, I've *often* told you about her. Her husband's the head of the Indian Cultural Centre in Osaka. They've lived in the Kansai for over thirty years. Mrs Prakash speaks fluent Japanese and she was interpreting for this other lady. We were learning about *pâté en croute*. I'm not sure you'd like it."

Hanae became silent, apparently troubled by indecision

about whether or not to try it on him some time, while Otani disposed of the last few stray noodles. "So?" he enquired at last.

Hanae looked quite startled. "So what?"

"So, what has all that got to do with bonsai?"

"Oh. I'm sorry. Yes, well, some of us were standing in the lobby talking afterwards and I may have brought the subject up by mentioning to Mrs Ebihara that you'd been made Chairman of the Rokko Bonsai Club –"

"Hanae! What a thing to boast about!"

Otani was honestly embarrassed, and Hanae coloured a little. "You may think that, but I'm very proud of you. And Mrs Ebihara can be so tiresome, going on all the time about her daughter who married the man who reads the news on Asahi TV."

Otani shook his head slowly. "And no doubt you'll be just as bad if it turns out to be true that *your* son-in-law's going to be a director of a department when they come back to Osaka. So this poor lady from India had to hear all about our little local bonsai club, did she?"

Still on the defensive, Hanae managed a touch of haughtiness. "She was very interested, as a matter of fact. You could see that from the way she reacted when Mrs Prakash told her in English. It seems all the well-off ladies in Bombay are going in for bonsai. It gives them an interest. They meet regularly in each other's houses and have talks about the various styles. Mrs Prakash's friend's got a weeping-cascade plum herself, and I told her about our lovely maple."

"Mrs Ebihara must have been thrilled." Otani stretched and shifted on his cushion, obscurely irritated by the idea of gaggles of well-to-do Indian ladies clucking over something so essentially Japanese as bonsai. It verged on the blasphemous, whereas he had been rather touched by the thought of a little band of English devotees making their way half-way round the world to the place in which their art found its highest expression. "Well. I think I'll just ring the duty room and see what's been happening. Then we'll look at the weather forecast, shall we?"

27

"I'm sure they'd have reported if there was anything serious, dear. Besides, you didn't mention why you had to have such a discussion about this fashion show. You don't normally take any interest in such things."

"It was Kimura who went on about it. I suppose he likes the idea of all these sophisticated foreign designers and glamorous models coming to Kobe. If I know him he'll manage to get acquainted with them one way or another. It does sound as though there'll be a lot of publicity. Apparently the people at the city hall are very excited about it."

"I don't quite understand what it all has to do with the police, though," Hanae said.

"Oh, we always need to know what's going on," her husband replied airily as he swung his legs out of the kotatsu pit and straightened his cotton yukata. "I enjoyed my dinner. Thank you. I will just make that call, after all. Won't be a minute."

As he made his way to the telephone in the kitchen Hanae studied his retreating back thoughtfully, wondering what he was keeping from her. She could always tell at once when he was being evasive.

Chapter IV

"Good Lord! It's Inspector Thing! I say, hang on a minute!" Kimura and Mie were passing the open gates of the Kobe Regatta and Athletic Club when the penetrating, half-remembered voice assailed his ears and he paused, puzzled. Two women in white tennis clothes were standing about fifty yards away by the open hatchback of a car in the forecourt of the clubhouse, one of them waving frantically.

"Who on earth is that?" Mie enquired, hanging back as recognition dawned in Kimura's face and he made to go in.

"It's an English lady I used to know," he said. "Mrs Byers-Pinkerton, but she tells people to call her Mrs B-P. Come on, I'll introduce you. You'll enjoy meeting her, she's quite a character. Her husband's something to do with insurance."

It was the third day after the passage of the typhoon which had done little material damage to the city itself, though there had been the usual flooding, and landslides in the hills. A number of advertising hoardings and lengths of fencing had been brought down, and an ornamental tree in front of the prefectural offices had been uprooted and had crushed the roof of a car parked nearby. A few of the people rash enough to have ventured out on foot during the height of the storm had been bruised or cut by flying debris, and one man was on the danger list with serious head injuries caused when he was struck by a tile dislodged from the roof of a house: there was no liability on the part of the householder, for the law was clear that pedestrians going out in a typhoon did so at their own risk. An old lady in Akashi, just to the west of Kobe, had died of heart failure when one of the storm shutters outside her house was suddenly blown away, but the local patrolman suggested delicately in his report that the daughter-in-law who summoned him from the neighbourhood police box was disposed to regard it as something of a blessing.

The glorious post-typhoon weather was a blessing of a wholly unambiguous kind. The sullen humidity of late summer had finally gone from the air, and everything looked fresh and sparkling, with only a few wisps of cloud trailing high above in a sky of a delicate, heart-lifting blue which had everyone drawing attention to the "autumn clarity" which all right-thinking Japanese regard as being peculiar to their homeland.

As Kimura and Mie approached the car he smiled with spontaneous pleasure at Sara Byers-Pinkerton, whom he had last seen disappearing round a street corner in clumsy confusion after planting an enthusiastic kiss on his face three years before; then recoiled slightly as she appeared to be about to do it again.

"Why, Mrs Byers-Pinkerton!" he exclaimed, hastily seizing her hand and pumping it vigorously. "What a delightful surprise! It's great to see you again. I'm Jiro Kimura," he added to her companion whose cool elegance presented a sharp contrast to Mrs B-P's flustered exuberance.

"You remember, Selena," she now burst out. "I wrote to you all about him when poor old Dotty kicked the bucket. Isn't he dishy? Douglas went about positively *glowering* with jealousy, you can see why, can't you? The master sleuth.

Sherlock Holmes couldn't hold a candle to this man. And perfect English, just like I told you. Hullo."

Her greeting to Mie Nakazato was distinctly perfunctory, and Mie's bow no more than polite, though she was relieved to observe that the bare legs under the abbreviated tennis skirt were on the beefy side, practically what are known rudely in Japan as "radish-legs". Furthermore, she must be at least forty in spite of her extrovert manner. On the other hand, the legs of the considerably younger woman called Selena were not only long and slender but much straighter than her own, and she also obviously intended her nipples to stick out like that under her soft white shirt.

"Let me introduce my friend Mie Nakazato," Kimura said. "She's a reporter on the local paper here. She understands a lot of English but she's a bit shy of using it." Mie smiled uncomprehendingly as Mrs Byers-Pinkerton addressed a few words of what might have been Japanese to her in an execrable accent.

"Gosh, what a coincidence," she went on, turning with relief to Kimura. "This is my cousin, you see. Selena Stoke-Lacy. She's on the women's page of this new paper, I can never remember the name. The one that fat man started and upset the unions. He makes his lorry drivers print it, or something. Not Robert Maxwell, the other one."

Kimura had no idea what she was talking about, and Selena Stoke-Lacy seemed disinclined to enlighten him when he grasped at the single straw he had been offered. "You're a journalist too, Miss Stoke-Lacy?"

"Some people seem to think so," was all she said.

It was the first time she had spoken, and her acid tone confirmed Kimura's inital impression of her as a taut, discontented woman for all her obvious physical attractiveness. An awkward little silence fell, and Kimura cast about for another subject. "Still keeping up with your tennis, I see," he said heartily after a while.

Sara Byers-Pinkerton pulled a comical face. "Don't make me laugh. I just whack a few about now and then. Hopeless as

31

ever, but at least I can keep it up for about half an hour. Not like jogging, eh? Those were the days." She chortled and made a few vague passes with the racket she was holding. "Watch it, Martina Navratilova, your doom is nigh! The Nip members – oops, done it again – the Japanese members here think we're bonkers to play in October, even on a lovely day like this. Where are you two off to, anyway?"

"Ah, yes. We must be getting along. We're on our way to the Tamahimeden – that big new building almost next door, near the hospital. I don't suppose you've heard yet, but there's going to be a very big fashion show there next month – "

"Well of course we know, you soppy ha'porth, what do you think Selena's doing here? Two birds with one stone, crafty cat. Holiday first, sponging off Douglas and me, then Our Special Correspondent in Kobe reports on the Japanese rag scene." Mrs B-P had lost none of her former effortless ability to undermine Kimura's normally serene pride in the idiomatic fluency of his command of the English language, and as he strained to comprehend he realised with added embarrassment that his own lips were moving slightly. Selena Stoke-Lacy, for her part, seemed entirely disposed to allow her cousin to speak for her, and was ignoring both Kimura and Mie as completely as it was possible for somebody standing immediately beside them to do.

"Oh, I see," Kimura said uncertainly when Mrs B-P paused to take a breath, and then turned to appeal to her cousin's profile. "Miss Stoke-Lacy is staying on to write about 'Mode International' for her paper?"

The younger woman appeared to come to a decision to be charitable, and looked at him properly for the first time. "That's the general idea, yes," she conceded. There was no softening of her expression, and Kimura's sensitive sexual antennae picked up a generalised contempt for men. Had Mie not been with him he would without conscious thought have taken up the challenge by setting out to charm her, for her off-putting style went with unquestionably good looks. Her

32

brown hair was cut crisply short, in a style which emphasised the delicate bone-structure of her head, and the slender neck rising up from the open collar of her shirt had something of the proud grace of a ballet dancer's.

"Fantastic! Well, I expect we'll see you around," he said. "As a matter of fact, Nakazato-san here is going to talk to one of the organisers in a few minutes' time about setting up interviews with some of the foreign participants, so we really must be on our way." Although Mie had neither spoken nor moved, Kimura was sharply conscious that she was ill at ease and anxious to get away from the two formidable foreigners. "It was great to talk to you again, Mrs Byers-Pinkerton," he added, beginning to turn away. "By the way, how's your dog? Clancy, isn't it?"

"Gladstone. He really liked you, didn't he? Oh, he's all right I suppose, lazy old sod. Here, you *are* still detecting away, I presume? How come you're so clued up on this fashion lark? I say, there isn't going to be a murder, is there?" All at once Mrs B-P opened her eyes very wide and her free hand flew briefly to her mouth as a dark flush began to mantle her neck and cheek. "Oh God," she groaned, "there I go again. It's just that you never think of famous detectives going out with girls. Specially lady reporters. Come on, Selena, we'd better push off before I put my big foot in it again.'

Even Selena's mouth twitched slightly as Mrs B-P flung her racket into the back of the car and then started rummaging busily in it, her sturdy bottom protruding. "That's right," Kimura said to her weakly. "Just walking my friend to her appointment. Your cousin has it a little wrong, anyway. I just kind of liaise with the foreign community here. So I'm naturally interested in a big international event like this show, quite apart from. . ."

"I can imagine," Selena said off-handedly. "Well, goodbye."

Mrs B-P's flushed face came into view again wearing an embarrassed grin. "Bye. Super to see you again. I can torment old Douglas now."

Mie remained silent until she and Kimura had gone out of

the gate and were approaching the Tamahimeden. "Excuse me," she then asked politely, "but have you had an affair with that lady?"

"An affair? With Mrs B-P? What an idea! Of course not. She's like that with everybody."

Mie looked unconvinced. "What's a *sopi hepaasu*? She called you a *sopi hepaasu*."

Kimura had no idea what "soppy ha'porth" meant either, and had barely even registered the phrase. "I can't imagine. To be quite honest, I don't understand a lot of what she says. It must be some out-of-date slang expression. I don't think she's lived in England for a good many years. Anyway, I assure you that I only interviewed her in the line of duty, and it never entered my head to – "

"Well, I'm sure it entered hers," Mie said firmly, and then smiled up at him radiantly. "I don't blame her, either." They had arrived at the main entrance to the Tamahimeden and both paused, reluctant to leave the mild sunshine. "The other lady's very attractive, isn't she?" Mie added a little wistfully as Kimura eyed her with appreciation.

Mie was twenty-four, and even since she had left her "office lady" job at the tea ceremony school and become a journalist he had never seen her less than beautifully groomed and made up. She had, however, begun to take tentative steps towards conformity with the very different dress code of media persons in Japan, and Kimura guessed that in view of the encounter with the two Englishwomen she must have been glad to be wearing a stylish outfit new to him: black wide cropped trousers with braces over a white shirt with a wing collar and a red tie.

He was right, but had no idea of the fuss her appearance had generated before she left the family home that morning. Observing her only daughter's descent into what she considered to be bohemianism of the most advanced kind, her snobbish mother in Kyoto feared the worst and was convinced that Mie's prospects of marriage must now be minimal. It was perhaps just as well that Mie had not mentioned her developing relationship with a police

34

inspector nearly twenty years her senior for fear of provoking a real crisis that probably need never arise. For she was well aware that she completely lacked the sort of sophistication that Western women like Selena Stoke-Lacy commanded so casually, and she had no illusions about the likely extent of Kimura's experience with such glamorous creatures. It was in fact something of a puzzle to her that he continued to seek her out, especially since she had gone to some pains to confirm discreetly that he had told her the truth when he announced that he was not married and never had been, and that he was not therefore in quest of a discreet extramarital fling. On the other hand Mie certainly gained no impression that he was looking for a wife, and for the moment was content to enjoy his company for its own sake without investing too much emotional capital in him.

"I'm sure you're wrong about Mrs B-P, but I'm very flattered anyway," Kimura said. "Thank you. As for the other one, well, she could be attractive if she didn't look so disagreeable all the time."

"Perhaps she's around fashion models a lot," Mie suggested. "The ones in the magazines often have that kind of expression on their faces." She looked at her watch. "I shall have to go in or I shall be late for my appointment with Mr Kinjo. Thank you for my lunch. Wish me luck, please."

Kimura was surprised; he often forgot how young Mie was. "Luck? You don't need any luck, he's the one who should be grateful. These people are always grateful for publicity." He stepped on the mat to make the automatic glass doors open for her. "Well, I must get back to the office myself. May I call you again soon? Good. Ciao."

As he re-passed the gates of the Kobe Regatta and Athletic Club Kimura glanced inside to see if the two women were still there, but there was no sign of the car. He shook his head with a little smile and continued on his way more purposefully than before. Walking Mie to the Tamahimeden and hearing her mention the name of Uehara's colourless henchman Kinjo had reminded him to chase up the threatening letter sent to Masako Yasuda.

35

Chapter V

MASAKO YASUDA MODES
Office of the Executive Secretary

Tokyo, October 18

Dear Inspector Kimura,
Forgive me if I dispense with the customary formalities in writing to you this hurried note to accompany a photocopy of the letter I mentioned to you when you were good enough to spare me some time after the meeting at the City Hall last week: I am sorry indeed that you had to remind our Kobe representative Mr Kinjo that I had failed to do this as I should have done immediately after my return to Tokyo. I am sure you will understand when I explain that Madame Yasuda would prefer to keep the original of the letter for the time being.

Let me reassure you that the letter has been examined by experts consulted on our behalf in confidence by the

36

director of a private detective agency which has undertaken work for us in the past. No fingerprints were found on it except those of Madame Yasuda's personal secretary who opened it, Madame Yasuda's own, and of course mine. Clearly the author took great pains to guard against its identification. Photocopies of the front and back of the envelope in which it arrived here are also enclosed.

No further communication of this kind has been received by us, and I have with some difficulty persuaded Madame Yasuda not to pay any of the money demanded. She is, however, understandably much distressed by this disturbing sequence of events, and with the approach of the deadline specified in the letter becomes daily more anxious. She asks me to express her personal appreciation of your kindness in agreeing to look into the matter.

Please let me or Mr Kinjo know if there is anything more I can do to help at this stage. As you know I plan to transfer my own base of operations to Kobe in a week or so.

Yours sincerely,
Hiroshi Uehara

"Well, what do you make of it, Hara-san?" Kimura waited more or less patiently as Inspector Hara of the Criminal Investigation Section laid the letter down, removed his glasses, polished them carefully with a piece of bright yellow cloth he produced from his pocket and which bore the words KURABAYASHI OPTICAL in English, replaced them and then blinked at him. "A curious communication in a number of ways, Inspector, but then the case as you have explained it to me exhibits unusual characteristics anyway, does it not?"

"All right. I agree it's a funny sort of letter. What particularly strikes you as odd about it?" Hara was a comparatively new member of the headquarters team, having transferred from Nagasaki the previous year, and Kimura had grudgingly come to respect his intellectual powers and his insatiable thirst for information on every subject, the more recondite the better. Hara's ponderous manner could be very

37

trying, though, and as he waited for him to marshal his thoughts Kimura found himself wondering yet again how on earth he had come to be such a crony of Noguchi's.

"It might perhaps be more constructive if I were to offer you my observations in the form of questions, Inspector." Hara was always meticulous over forms of address. "One could draw up a considerable list." He heaved a sigh and assumed the mournful look he always wore when thinking aloud. "In the first place, why did Uehara not send the original letter? Why, having sought you out to tell you about the letter, did he put off sending you even this copy? Why has a fashion house found it necessary to have recourse in the past to the services of a private detective agency, and one moreover with access to technical resources of a reasonably sophisticated nature? Why in any case were the Tokyo police not consulted at the outset? Your judgement is that Mr Uehara is an able, sophisticated man. He must also be intellectually arrogant to a degree if he supposes that this flimsy excercise in deception is likely to take you in."

"Deception? Aren't you rather jumping to conclusions?" Kimura was startled by Hara's unqualified scepticism. Hara picked up the photocopy which lay beside Uehara's letter on Kimura's desk and blinked at it furiously for a few seconds.

"Two hundred thousand American dollars," he said with a smile which irritated Kimura. "An 'insurance premium'. The letter obviously produced on a word-processor using one of the several software programmes which can combine Japanese and English in the same text. Masako Yasuda Modes is no doubt equipped with microcomputers and printers as well as quite possibly a more elaborate system. If it were worth it, it would be a relatively simple matter to check this against samples produced by their printers, for each will of course have its distinctive characteristics, just as type-writers have. I should not, you see, be in the least surprised if the original of this document proves to have been produced on the Yasuda premises. Mr Uehara has at least refrained from being so insulting as to have his own letter to you

38

produced by the same machine." He replaced the photocopy and leant over to peer more closely at Uehara's signature. "I like his calligraphy. He has of course used one of the handy plastic 'brush pens' rather than a traditional brush and ink, but I don't myself object to them for everyday use."

"Decent of you to say so," Kimura said, thoroughly nettled. "I'll let Uehara know next time I see him. Look here, Hara, I'm not completely naive, you know. It has of course occurred to me that Uehara or even Masako Yasuda herself might have dreamed all this up as a neat way to milk the official accounts of the firm and squirrel away some money in a personal hidey-hole outside the country by paying off some entirely mythical extortioners. I see the force of your questions – most of them, anyway. Just assuming for the purposes of discussion that there really have been menacing phone calls and that the letter is genuine, though, there could be reasonable answers to them. It could be that Uehara was not in fact authorised by Masako Yasuda to raise the matter with me, and that he had a hard job persuading her afterwards that he'd done the right thing. That could account for the delay and for her refusal to part with the original letter. It could also explain why they hadn't been to the Tokyo police. The detective agency contact I don't find in the least surprising. You know as well as I do that big companies frequently pay agencies to run confidential checks on job applicants. You know, keeping out people with the wrong sort of family background and so forth."

Kimura raised a warning hand as he saw Hara's mouth opening, warding off what he felt sure was to be a lecture on the social and economic discrimination still widely practised against the former outcast families of the *burakumin* ghettoes. "OK, Yasuda Modes may not be a big company in the accepted sense of employing a lot of people. All the same it's a very well-known enterprise, and I would guess that in the world of high fashion people guard their design ideas very carefully indeed. Their staff could be vulnerable to approaches – or of course it could just as well work the other

39

way, with Yasuda hiring private enquiry agents to snoop around and report what her competitors are up to." He looked sternly at Hara's moon face, quite carried away by the flood of his own eloquence.

Hara nodded judiciously. "Your points are well taken, Inspector. It would appear that only time will tell whether or not there is a genuine attempt at extortion here. The envelope which your friend Mr. Uehara has also been thoughtful enough to have photocopied for you tells us nothing, of course, beyond the fact that the Yasuda address has been typed in Roman script, that the letter was posted some time in the afternoon of the third of October at the Central Post Office in Kobe, and that the sender paid the surcharge for priority delivery. Needless to say, and in contravention of the postal regulations, there is no sender's address on the reverse."

"The post code has been written in by hand, of course," Kimura pointed out. Envelopes used for Japanese domestic mail are sold in approved standard sizes, and to facilitate machine sorting have three larger and two smaller boxes printed in red on the bottom right-hand side on the front for the addressee's postal zone numbers. The two little boxes are for subsidiary zone numbers generally needed only for rural districts. "But a graphologist couldn't do much with just three digits."

"Just so. Well, Inspector, beyond reiterating my suggestion to you that Uehara is, with or without the collusion of Madame Yasuda, paving the way for a discreet embezzlement of company funds, there appears to be nothing I can do to assist you." Hara placed his hands on the arms of the visitor's chair in Kimura's tiny cubicle of an office as though to take his leave, but Kimura put up a hand.

"Don't go just yet if you can spare another minute or two," he said. "It's helpful to have your reactions." Kimura spoke no more than the simple truth. For all Hara's schoolmasterly prolixity, his immediate and forthright dismissal of the whole affair as a put-up job had jolted his own thinking into a new

40

frame of reference, and he wanted to take the discussion further.

With a courteous gesture, Hara subsided again into his chair. "I am at your disposal," he murmured, and Kimura leaned forward in his own chair.

"Thank you. Right. Time will tell, you said. As I see it, there are two, maybe three possible scenarios over the next couple of weeks. First, Yasuda decides to pay the money before the deadline. That would be easy enough to check in Tokyo. I mean, they couldn't transfer such a sum and cover it up – pretend they didn't. In any case, there'd be no point in attempting to if your theory is correct. So. The so-called 'premium' having been paid, nothing else happens except that the lucky holder of the numbered Swiss account – whose identity the Swiss bank certainly won't reveal to us – is a couple of hundred thousand dollars better off. If Yasuda's accountants are any good at their job, the loss will be offset against tax. A nice, tidy outcome. You agree?"

"That is precisely the, ah, 'scenario' I envisage," Hara agreed gravely.

Kimura raised two fingers. "Scenario Two. They don't pay. The deadline passes." He extended a finger of the other hand. "Variant One. Nothing happens. Extortion attempt revealed as a bluff, but in that event the assumption must be that it was 'genuine' at least in the sense of not having been dreamed up by Uehara with or without Yasuda's complicity."

"Or alternatively that Uehara lacked the confidence to carry the thing through."

"Okay. I agree. Now Variant Two." Kimura put up another finger, studied the result and then in some confusion put his hands out of Hara's sight. "Variant Two. Something *does* happen, who knows what, short of real disaster but nevertheless fairly disagreeable, as a kind of warning that the extortioner means business and they'd better pay up or else. This would neither prove nor disprove the existence of a real extortioner, let's call him Mister X. It could well be that if Uehara is himself Mister X he might use a ploy like that to add a touch of realism to his scheme – "

"Precisely. The script would then revert to that for your Scenario One. One could of course devise other variants, but I think you have established very clearly the nature of the dilemma in which you find yourself. What precisely do you propose to do at this stage, Inspector?"

Kimura began to scratch his head in a gesture of puzzlement much favoured by Japanese schoolboys and which he knew most of his woman friends found extremely appealing, but desisted when he noticed the look of distaste on Hara's face. "I'm not too sure," he admitted. "Any ideas? You're the head detective around here."

Hara raised a pudgy hand to his mouth and coughed discreetly. "How kind of you to put it like that," he said. "I had supposed. . .well, let it pass. Suffice it to say that I am flattered to be consulted. It would appear that, as is so often the case with our work, the way forward – if you are disposed to devote time and energy to this affair – is by way of the patient accumulation of information. The Tokyo police should be apprised of the situation, for if my view of the matter is correct it will fall to the metropolitan force to investigate the matter in due course. In the meantime our colleagues there would no doubt be good enough to pass on informally what they know about both Mr. Uehara and Madam Yasuda. Also perhaps their liaison officer currently in Kobe, Mr Kinjo. It would be interesting to know if Mr Kinjo was in Kobe on the third of this month, for reasons which will be obvious to you, and if possible discreetly to obtain a specimen of typing from his temporary office at the Tamahimeden. You will I presume as a matter of course enquire into the financial structure of Masako Yasuda Modes and the identities of the principal shareholders in the company. Unfortunately, only if there were satisfactory *prima facie* evidence of actual fraud or other criminal activity would the district prosecutor consent to an approach to banks in Tokyo to establish whether any individual associated with the company had arranged transfers in the past to this particular numbered account in Switzerland. However, I

42

would think it unlikely. The owner of the account is probably discreet enough to be in the habit of going to Europe to make deposits in cash."

Kimura looked at him in some awe. "You wouldn't like to take this on, I suppose, would you?"

Hara smiled sweetly and shook his head. "You are most kind to suggest it, but I must decline. As I have already suggested, I rather doubt whether it is at present a matter for the Hyogo force at all. Still less would I presume to take the lead in a case which, if it does indeed develop along disturbing lines here in Kobe, could involve the interests and wellbeing of distinguished foreign visitors. I am quite sure that Superintendent Otani would not at all approve of my doing so."

Hara hauled himself to his feet and loomed over Kimura, who remained in his chair. "Please be assured that I shall be delighted to discuss the matter with you at any time, and of course offer the full cooperation of my section should you require it." He paused and then spoke with uncharacteristic simplicity. "What is it that's bothering you so much about this business? Is it really worth your time?"

There was silence for several seconds as Kimura looked up at him. "You haven't met Uehara," he said at last. "I have. He's a smooth character, certainly. But when he spoke to me about this, I think he was a frightened man."

Chapter VI

Although his view of the main entrance was obscured not only by the figure of his driver Tomita holding the door open for him but also by the umbrella he was brandishing protectively against the dismal drizzle, Otani, as he clambered out of his official car, gained the impression that Kimura was not altogether pleased with the man he was evidently seeing off the premises. Not that there was anything remarkable about the curt little bow with which his assistant acknowledged the much deeper one made by the departing visitor, nor anything obviously distasteful about the man, to all appearances a conventional middle-aged office worker of some kind. He was probably in his early fifties, and was wearing a drably respectable "salaryman" suit, over which he was pulling an equally unremarkable gabardine topcoat as he made his way down the front steps of the shabby old building which was Otani's second home.

Brushing aside the umbrella the faithful Tomita urged on him, Otani sprinted up the steps in time to see Kimura's back disappearing through the swing doors at the back of the lobby. "Inspector! A moment, if you don't mind?" At the sound of the familiar voice Kimura wheeled round at once and pulled himself up smartly, mainly for the benefit of the decrepit former patrolman who was during normal office hours the Hyogo prefectural police force's second line of headquarters defence, after the man in riot gear posted outside. The old man was laboriously logging his commander into the tattered exercise book he insisted on maintaining years after that ancient practice had been officially superseded. Headstrong and rackety as he was, Kimura believed that it would never do for it to become generally known that the superintendent permitted even his most senior subordinates to get away with sloppy discipline.

"Sir!" he therefore barked efficiently, suppressing a quick grin as he saw Otani's right eyelid flicker in what he was fairly sure was a conspiratorial wink.

"Ah, Inspector, I thought it was you. I wonder if, when it is convenient of course, you would drop into my office for a few minutes?"

"Of course, sir. May I accompany you there right away?"

Otani nodded gravely. "I should be much obliged."

The old doorkeeper watched approvingly as the two men mounted the broad stairs to the first floor, Kimura a respectful two steps behind. Once round the bend of the landing Kimura skipped up to Otani's side and they strolled together down the broad corridor with its strip of coconut matting down the middle towards Otani's office. About halfway, Otani paused and contemplated one of the framed photographs of his predecessors which lined the grubby whitewashed walls. "Eleventh till the fifteenth year of Showa," he read aloud reflectively, then turned to look at Kimura. "Fifty years ago, when I was just a boy. Long before you were born, Kimura-kun. Think yourself lucky you'll never have to wear a uniform like that."

Kimura peered at the grim face in the photograph and nodded. "Either his collar's strangling him or he's suffering from constipation," he said irreverently.

"Or possibly an uneasy conscience," Otani suggested, then smiled faintly as Kimura raised an eyebrow in some surprise. "There's a family connection," he explained. "He was the one who did most of the questioning of my father. Normally the head of the prefectural police wouldn't have involved himself personally in a 'dangerous thoughts' enquiry. But my father was a full professor of Osaka Imperial University, after all – "

"And a very distinguished scientist – "

"And some kind of cousin by marriage," Otani went on, ignoring the interruption. "I suppose I might even have met him, without realising it, before my father got himself into trouble by saying the wrong things. Strange to think that my picture will go up on this same wall before all that long." He made a sound half-way between a sigh and a chuckle, and then briskly covered the last few yards to his office, giving Kimura barely time to reach it ahead of him and hold the door open.

"What had your visitor said to upset you?" Otani said as he hung his braided hat on the old-fashioned wooden coat and umbrella stand and gestured Kimura to his usual seat. "Who was he, anyway?"

Kimura cleared his throat before replying a little stiffly. "It was a man called Kinjo. Fumio Kinjo. He's representing Yasuda Modes – that's Masako Yasuda's company of course – here until her man Uehara arrives to handle all the administration for the big fashion show next month. I wasn't upset, Chief."

"Yes, you were."

"I was *not* upset," Kimura insisted with mounting irritation as he saw Otani's lips twitch.

Then a smile briefly lit up Otani's swarthy face. "You sound like that American tennis player on the television," he said. "All right, Kimura, have it your own way. It's nothing to do with me, anyway. Since I've dragged you up here, though, fill me in on the business of that other American. The business man. You know, the fellow whose house was shot up

46

accidentally by those two yakuza on motorbikes last spring. Did we pay for the repairs in the end? The district prosecutor mentioned the affair casually when I was talking to him earlier today about something else, and I couldn't remember the details."

Kimura nodded glumly. "Yes, both times," he said. "I really feel sorry for Mr Riley, living just across the street from the boss of the Ichiwa gang while the feud's still going on. The gang accepted that the stray bullets were meant for them and offered to pay for the hole in the Rileys' fence and the damage inside their house, but Hara's people had to dig the bullets out as evidence and what with one thing and another we ended up with the bill. The second time it was one of our own bullets that went though the Rileys' upstairs window and wrecked a portable radio belonging to their son. Just as well he was at school when the opposition came barrelling down the road in that dump truck for another try and our men on guard outside fired back. All we could do was apologise and pay up." He sighed. "At least Ninja tells me the word has gone out to all concerned to lay off that particular house in future. The gangs are as keen to keep foreigners out of all this as we are."

Otani nodded in approval. The appointed successor to the old patriarch who had formerly dominated organised crime in western Japan had not lasted long before being gunned down by followers of his principal rival, and in less than a year the resulting schism had claimed the lives of over a dozen gangsters, with five innocent citizens wounded by stray bullets. The Hyogo police had lost face alarmingly over the damage to the Riley residence, but thank goodness the American family had suffered no personal injuries: the Japanese victims of the gang warfare at least understood these things and accepted their compensation without too much fuss.

"Oh, well. It's all very worrying, but we do have other things to do as well," Otani said. "What did this Kinjo man want? I strolled over to the Tamahimeden the other day and had a look round, by the way. Just out of curiosity. A

47

Rotarian friend of mine's on the board of the company that owns it. Something like that. He showed me round."

Kimura sat back and looked at him warily as Otani rambled on. Though he would have preferred to wait until he had thought it over, he realised that the Old Man was determined to hear about his meeting with Kinjo before he left the room. "It really is extraordinary. One of the reception rooms I saw has a little balcony. Apparently for an extra fee the newly-weds can make an appearance on it during the reception surrounded by a pink cloud. Made with stuff they use in theatres, I believe. If that's the sort of performance people go in for nowadays I'm not surprised you're still a bachelor."

It had been a very long time since Otani had last seriously offered to do something about finding Kimura a bride, and although he continued to tease him about his single state Kimura no longer reacted defensively. "Yes, it's quite a place," he said flatly.

"The Yasuda people have an office there already, do they?" Otani enquired with an air of innocence, and Kimura sat up straight as he nodded.

"Yes. Kinjo's there on his own for the moment. Not that there can be a great deal for him to do before Uehara arrives. They can handle most of the preparations perfectly well from their Tokyo headquarters."

"Did you ask Kinjo to come here today, or was it his idea?"

"I asked him. I wanted to explore some lines of enquiry that suggested themselves when Hara and I had a talk about this alleged extortion attempt. I thought it would be no bad idea to have Kinjo here and lean on him a little bit."

Otani began to reach into his pocket for a cigarette, but then pulled a face and stopped himself. "You implied a moment ago that he probably doesn't have a great deal to occupy his time. Have you considered that he might have been sent here to negotiate with whoever's behind the threatening letters and phone calls?"

The notion had in fact first entered Kimura's head not much more than half an hour earlier, during his unsatisfactory conversation with Kinjo. "Of course I have, Chief," he said with a touch of indignation. "I may say that Hara's inclined to pooh-pooh the whole idea. He thinks it's a scheme cooked up by Uehara to squirrel away some money for himself. Embezzlement, in effect."

Otani nodded. "I see. Imaginary extortioners. Well, Hara could be right, you know. It wouldn't be the first time that sort of thing's been tried. Did you get any indications one way or the other from Kinjo?"

Kimura twisted his lips into an upside-down smile and shrugged. "Not really. You were right of course, Chief. Must have eyes in the back of your head. I was feeling rather frustrated when you saw me with him. Whatever might or might not be going on, Kinjo's a funny sort of customer. I rang a friend of mine in the Met and they ran a quick check for me. Kinjo doesn't have any record, but judging by his tax returns he's a drifter, never worked for one company for more than a few years, and I wouldn't mind betting he's done a few shady deals in his time. Kinjo himself told me he'd spent most of his life in the public relations and advertising business, but he doesn't have the personality to be a front man. My guess is that he used to sell space in magazines, that sort of thing. Hardly suitable for an up-market outfit like Yasuda Modes, I should have thought."

"How long has he been with them?" Knowing nothing about the world of high fashion, Otani did not presume to question Kimura's judgement openly, but privately considered that he was being a little naive.

"About four years, he said, but I couldn't find out whether he was recruited by her or by Uehara. I can only assume that he's employed basically as some kind of general fixer and odd-job man. Certainly I'd say he's capable of acting as a go-between if somebody really is putting the squeeze on the firm and they seriously want to negotiate. The trouble is that although he says he's heard rumours about some sort of pressure being put on Yasuda he insists he hasn't been taken into her confidence – or Uehara's. And in a letter he sent me just the other day Uehara said Masako Yasuda had decided to tough it out and refuse to pay. Reluctantly, he said."

Otani stretched in his chair and stifled a yawn, "Well, it all sounds quite complicated enough even for you, Kimura. I must say I don't care much for the sound of Madame Yasuda's set-up, and judging by the Wakamatsu Department Store deal she screwed out of her former boy-friend she must be quite wily enough to avoid being taken for a ride by anybody else. It might be worth keeping a discreet eye on Kinjo while he's on his own down here, I suppose. Ninja's very busy trying to contain this wretched gang warfare, but by the same token the yakuza are squabbling so much among themselves that they're tempted into indiscretions. He might hear something if Kinjo is in touch with any of them. When does the rest of the circus arrive, by the way?"

Kimura took out his diary and flipped through the pages. "Uehara and the technical people are due quite soon, but the rest of them and the foreigners won't be here until the big press conference scheduled for the afternoon of the fourth of next month. That's a couple of days before the gala preview of the actual show."

Otani stood up and crossed to his desk where he looked at his own forward diary. "Well, I really do hope nothing troublesome happens, Kimura," he said after a while. "That's just when the bonsai delegation from England is going to be around, and I'm hoping to see something of them."

He rubbed his hands briskly as Kimura correctly inferred that he was being dismissed from the presence. "As I said, I don't think we need lose too much sleep over the idea of Masako Yasuda being possibly taken for a ride. Just make sure we aren't, Kimura-kun."

Chapter VII

"*Moshi-moshi!* Is that Inspector Kimura? Ah. It's Uehara here. Mode International. Returning your call. Sorry I wasn't available when you rang this morning. As you can imagine, things are pretty chaotic this end. . . What's that? Under control? Well, I suppose you could put it like that. Nobody's pulled out, anyway. . .Why, yes, didn't Kinjo-san tell you? The day after tomorrow. . .Yes, it certainly will. And besides, there's a lot of technical stuff to organise on the spot. . .I beg your pardon? This isn't a very good line. . .Oh. Oh yes, I'm sorry. . .Yes, I know I did. And the deadline was today, yes. Anyway, it's no deal. . .No, I wouldn't say I persuaded her. Madame Yasuda can be pretty tough when people try to put anything over on her, and the decision was hers. I'm just keeping my fingers crossed. You haven't picked up any rumours in Kobe, have you?. . .No, I'm sure you and your colleagues are right, it never did sound like one of the gangs. They'd have approached us more openly. . .Yes, let's hope it was just a try-on by some crazy. . .Oh, you did?

51

That's fine. I hope you can be there. And stick around afterwards, we're planning an informal drinks party and you'll be able to meet everyone personally. . .Yes, of course I will, but I'm hoping we've heard the last of it. I'm sorry if Kinjo hasn't been much help to you. Still, as of the day after tomorrow I'll be right there at the Tamahimeden myself. Thank you, Inspector. We appreciate your advice. Right. *Yoroshiku.*"

Kimura put the phone down and rubbed his ear thoughtfully as he looked again at the expensively embossed invitation card for the Mode International press conference which had arrived through the post that day. He wished he could have seen Uehara's face as well as hearing his voice over the telephone. The news that Masako Yasuda had decided in the end against paying protection money came as something of a surprise to him, because by then Kimura had come round very much to Hara's way of thinking. To invent an imaginary extortioner as a means of siphoning off a small fortune from the Yasuda accounts struck him as an ingenious ploy, and one that the slick Uehara, with or without the help of his shifty assistant Kinjo, might well be able to carry off with panache and conviction. It seemed that Hara was mistaken, though.

Kimura shrugged and decided to reserve further judgement on the whole affair. Uehara was due to arrive in Kobe within forty-eight hours, and could fight his own battles, if any. He decided he would definitely go along to the press conference and the promised party, though, and carefully entered the date and time in his pocket diary, then picked up the invitation card and slipped it back into its envelope and tossed it into the Pending tray on his desk.

He stretched luxuriously, yawned, stood up and had begun to move towards the door before he suddenly froze, turned back and picked up the invitation again, staring at it as he felt his way back into his chair, unlocked the drawer and pulled out the photocopies of the letter and envelope which Uehara had sent him and he had shown to Hara. His invitation to the press conference bore a Kobe postmark: obviously Kinjo had sent them out. His name and official address were handwritten in Japanese rather than typed as in the case of the envelope which had allegedly contained the demand for protection money.

Kimura had only the numerals written in the post-code boxes to compare, and spent a long time doing so.

Chapter VIII

"Look, there's Kuniko Doi!" Mie whispered excitedly to Kimura as the double doors were flung open and a mixed group of Japanese and foreigners festooned with huge beribboned artifical chrysanthemums, similar to the rosettes worn in England only by election candidates and prize beasts at agricultural shows, were shepherded into one of the smaller reception rooms at the Tamahimeden wedding hall. A long table had been placed at one end with chairs for a dozen or so, and a double-sided name card done in both Roman and Japanese script had been positioned by each. Nevertheless, there was some initial confusion as people bumped into each other and apologised while trying to find their places, and it was a minute or two before they had all sorted themselves out. Meantime Uehara and Masako Yasuda remained by the open doors in murmured conference.

"In person," Kimura agreed indulgently as the eminent television personality detached herself from a little clot of foreigners and slid neatly into her seat. "They must be paying her a fortune to do the commentaries for the shows." The Mode International press conference had attracted a considerable gathering of reporters and photographers, and something like fifty people were sitting on flimsy gilt chairs arranged in half a dozen rows facing the top table. Several of them had cameras or tape recorders on their laps, but there was also a goodly crowd of professional photographers who had spurned the offer of chairs and were busy with their paraphernalia all over the room. Kansai Television had sent a camera crew, and people blinked and shielded their faces from time to time as they tested their powerful supplementary lights.

"Quite a turn-out," he went on, turning in his chair to have a good look round and waving cheerily to Selena Stoke-Lacy, who was seated beside an elderly, stick-like Western woman with a haggard face, her mouth a gash of glossy lipstick. Selena inclined her head in frosty acknowledgement. "Including quite a few foreigners. Mostly journalists based in Tokyo of course, but I believe there are several who've come specially from the States and Europe, like Miss Stoke-Lacy over there. You remember her with Mrs B-P at the tennis club. Representing *Vogue* and so on I suppose. Ah, it seems to be getting under way."

Masako Yasuda had taken her place and Uehara was clearing his throat noisily into a microphone placed beside a lectern to one side of the long table. In deference to the foreign guests he spoke first in English and then repeated his remarks in Japanese sentence by sentence. Most of the people in the room paid no particular attention to either version of his speech of welcome, and the babble of general conversation continued more or less unabated until Uehara proceeded to introduce those seated at the table.

As their names were mentioned the Japanese rose to their feet and bowed solemnly to the assembled company, while the foreign designers and the American, British and French diplomatic representatives tended to assume an ungainly crouching position half in and half out of their chairs, grinning sheepishly as the flash-bulbs popped and each received a perfunctory round of applause. On the other hand, and although relegated to the extreme ends of the table, the models Barbi Mingus and Vanessa Radley comported themselves with marvellous hauteur.

"You ought to do interviews with those two girls as well as the designers," Kimura murmured to Mie as Uehara invited the ladies and gentlemen of the media to put their questions to the visitors. "You know, something about the private lives of top international models. Look at the expression on Kuniko Doi's face – I wonder what she's thinking?"

Having glanced again through the photographs in the original information pack, Kimura could have identified the leading lights at the press conference without needing to look at their name-cards. It was interesting all the same to see them in the flesh for the first time, and he looked forward to meeting them over the informal drinks which Uehara had told him were due to follow the question-and-answer session. Kimura already knew two of the foreigners sitting at the long table. The British Consul-General had turned up from Osaka for the occasion, while the Americans were officially represented by a consul who was a particular friend of Kimura's. Both men were wearing professionally bland expressions of courteous attentiveness. The French envoy was new to him, not surprisingly since his name-plate indicated that he was the cultural counsellor from the Embassy in Tokyo. Kimura thought he looked more like a dress designer himself, in his Issaye Miyake jump-suit, than the soberly dressed Jean-Claud Villon. His hair was a jungle of unruly curls and he was also notably more animated than the average diplomat, his slightly protuberant eyes rolling in his red face as he whispered throughout the proceedings with seemingly equal urgency alternately to Villon and to his other neighbour Kuniko Doi, who for her part was obviously much more interested in Vanessa Radley, sitting and smouldering decoratively on her right.

Questions were slow in coming, few in number and banal in content, being mostly concerned with the foreign visitors' impressions of Japan, Japanese people and Japanese cuisine, with particular reference to raw fish. Kimura admired Uehara's interpreting, while gratified to note that it was not as skilful as his own. In spite of Uehara's efforts the session limped on unimpressively, until after a particularly awkward pause Masako Yasuda responded hesitantly and with becomingly modest idealism to a flattering, obviously planted question about her motives in organising Mode International in the first place and in choosing Kobe in which to stage it.

Hearing her voice for the first time, Kimura was struck by its girlishly high, breathy quality. It reminded him of the almost unbearably winsome intonation of the "nightingale girls" whose tape-recorded voices incessantly advise passengers on buses all over Japan of the name of the next stop, warn them that the driver may have to apply the brakes suddenly, and beg them neither to leave any "forgotten things" on board when they alight, nor to cross the road without first looking carefully in both directions. It was the more disconcerting because Madame Yasuda, though expertly made up, seemed otherwise content to act her age – her regal manner would in fact have been more suitable to a *grande dame* ten or twenty years her senior. Recalling that she had not uttered a word during the initial briefing at Kobe City Hall on the day of the typhoon, Kimura concluded that she had little taste for public speaking.

Silence fell again, but when Kimura nudged her and suggested that she should ask a question Mie blushed and shook her head violently. She had been quite embarrassed enough when on arriving for the press conference and spotting her Kimura had efficiently detached her from two more senior *Kobe Shimbun* reporters and their photographer colleague and planted himself in the chair next to her. In any case after a moment or two longer the cameramen suddenly seemed to reach an unspoken agreement like a flock of birds, and unceremoniously departed after the manner of their kind. Uehara sensibly took their exodus as a signal to bring the formal proceedings to an end and to invite those remaining to move to an adjoining room for refreshments and an opportunity to speak individually to the members of what he referred to in English as "the Mode International team".

"Hello there, Jiro!" Mie seized the chance to disengage her elbow from Kimura's hand and slip away to rejoin her colleagues on the other side of the room as the American consul bore down on them, a glass of gin and tonic in his hand. "I don't know about 'Mode International team'. I sat there thinking we must look a lot like that famous picture of The Last Supper people are so attached to in Japan. Remember the fuss the missionaries made when that steak house in Tokyo used it for an ad?"

Kimura stuck out a hand. "Bob, good to see you. Quite an occasion." He had known and liked Bob Froman for a long time.

Froman looked at him quizzically. "So. I know why I'm here. A drink's a drink even at four p.m. What's a nice guy like you doing in a place like this, though?"

"I have no secrets from you, Bob. I came to look at the models," Kimura said. "And of course to meet the famous Marian Norton. Will you introduce me?"

"I wouldn't recommend it, Jiro. She's a pain in the ass. Why don't I –"

"Pain in the arse? This whole thing's a pain in the arse if you ask me."

There was just time for Kimura to register the unmistakably British accent and the camp enunciation before the newcomer pushed his way past two Japanese anxiously conferring over a tape they were playing back on a miniature recorder and seized him by the elbow. "Terry Phipps. Oops, dear, so sorry, I thought you might be English."

"No, he's a card-carrying Japanese," Froman said comfortably. "But not such a frightfully bad sort all the same, don't you know." As Phipps looked at Froman warily Kimura noticed that his eyes were bloodshot.

58

"Not taking the piss, are you ducky? Don't bother. I tell you, I've had it up to *here* today. With Her Ladyship. And that harpy Tracy. So don't start, there's a dear." He wheeled back to Kimura. "Such *marvellous* English. You could have fooled me. Are you a friend of His Nibs? Yasuda's minder?"

"Who, Uehara? Not specially, but I know him of course. My name's Jiro Kimura."

"He's a –"

"I'm with one of the journalists from the *Kobe Shimbun* newspaper," Kimura continued smoothly over Froman's attempted interjection, noting gratefully that Froman subsided at once, however puzzled he might have been by Kimura's reluctance to be identified as a policeman.

Froman tried a different tack. "Who's been upsetting you, Mr Phipps?"

"Terry, dear."

"Terry, then. And who's Tracy?"

Phipps turned his eyes heavenwards and then pointed towards Wesley Wilberforce, who was standing to one side with Vanessa Radley, nodding gravely at something she was saying. In his dark grey pinstriped suit and waistcoat "Her Ladyship" looked like a bank manager about to turn down a request for an overdraft.

"Seventeen years at her beck and call. Body and soul. And there's no need to look at me like that. The body might not be up to much these days but I used to be able to take my pick once upon a time, let me tell you." Phipps paused long enough to direct a venomous look in the direction of his employer. "Well, one more little tantrum from *her* and that's it, it's pastures new for little me. It's not as if I haven't got some really *nice* friends to turn to. As for Tracy, did you *see* the way that ghastly old dyke showing off her bum in the trouser suit was drooling over her? Honestly, I could hardly stop *blushing*."

"I thought that was Vanessa Radley," Kimura said.

"Well, she could hardly go on the agency books as Tracy Pratt, could she ducky? Like poor old Diana Dors, bless her, *née* Fluck. She opened a vicarage fete once and the parson got confused and introduced her as Miss Diana Clunt better known as Dors. Who *is* that creature, anyway ?"

Froman was grinning happily at Phipps. "Hey, you're better than a weekend in Hong Kong, Terry," he said when the little Englishman finally paused for breath. "You should have paid attention to the introductions. Kuniko Doi is her name, and she'd be flattered to hear what you said about her. She runs a TV chat show for women only four afternoons a week. She's kind of a professional lesbian. Makes no secret of it, comes on pretty strong whenever she gets a good-looking guest on the show, and gets more fan-mail from bored housewives than you could shake a stick at. And as I suspect you know perfectly well, she's been hired to do the commentaries for Mode International. Japanese *and* English. She's not in Jiro's league but she can handle a script in English well enough."

Kimura nodded in agreement. It was a fair summary of Kuniko Doi's style and reputation, and he noticed that she was living up to it by gazing hungrily into Selena Stoke-Lacy's eyes as they both listened to something Marian Norton was saying to the skeletal woman who had been beside Selena in the audience.

In spite of the availability of drinks and canapés, by no means all of the Japanese journalists had stayed on after the press conference, and there were roughly equal numbers of Japanese and foreigners in the room. Their inhibitions lowered by alcohol, the Japanese media people had begun to approach the visiting celebrities, each of whom was now at the centre of a little clump of admirers. In Tsutomu Kubota's case these were mostly the younger among the women, though Kimura noted that Villon had also attracted some of these, including Mie. The colourful French cultural counsellor appeared to be interpreting for him, and to be attracting almost as much attention as Villon himself. The room was becoming very warm, and the air was laden with a mingling of expensive perfumes and cigarette smoke.

60

The decibel count was rising by the minute and it was hard for Kimura to catch everything Phipps was saying while glancing round the room now and then. He gave up the attempt to follow the conversation about Kuniko Doi altogether when he saw Uehara push his way through to Kubota, say something to him with an air of urgency and then almost at once take him by the arm and lead him towards Masako Yasuda who was by then standing near the middle of the room talking to a man who stood facing her. As her assistant and the Frenchman approached, Madame Yasuda smiled and took a half-step towards them. The other man also turned and the light from the elaborate central chandelier almost directly above illuminated his face for the first time.

Kimura was struck by the way he seemed to stand out in such a gathering. Glimpsed in a partially curtained car in the business centre of Osaka, or at a meeting of the Chamber of Commerce and Industry, he would not have rated a second glance. Stocky in build and wearing an obviously expensive but unfashionably cut navy-blue suit with a company badge winking in his lapel, he was probably at least sixty, yet there was an aura of driving, sensual energy about him. The skin of his face was swarthy, coarse and pitted; his expression that of a man accustomed to having his own way. He was in short the classic successful self-made Japanese businessman, and Kimura realised that he could only be Yutaka Watanabe, Masako Yasuda's former patron, present associate and the beleaguered president of the Wakamatsu chain of department stores.

Kimura was fairly sure that Watanabe had not been present at the press conference proper, and was just turning back to tune himself in again to the lively conversation still going on between Froman and Phipps when the chandelier fell on the businessman's head.

Chapter IX

"No, I've already told you," Kimura said testily, raising his hands to massage the tense muscles at the sides of his neck. "I was turning away when it happened, and only saw it out of the corner of my eye. It was no more than an impression, but for what it's worth I thought Uehara tried to pull Watanabe *out* of harm's way, not the reverse. It was confusing, because Ninja's friend Kubota seemed to be pushing Masako Yasuda out from under at the same time. Presumably Watanabe will be able to tell us for himself when he's fit to be questioned."

"There's no doubt he will be all right, is there?" Otani inquired. He had been about to leave for home when Inspector Hara had rung through from the duty room to report Kimura's call from the Tamahimeden, but decided to wait for his return and talk to Kimura himself. It was now after seven-thirty, but like every other bourgeois Japanese husband he was sublimely confident that whatever time he arrived home his wife would quickly produce his dinner without complaint.

"I've come straight from the Kaigan Hospital. It's practically next door to the Tamahimeden, as you know. Just as well. That chandelier must weigh at least twenty-five kilos. A few inches difference and it could easily have broken his neck. As it is, they think he'll pull through. There's a hairline fracture of the skull and they had to put something like thirty stitches into his scalp. And of course he's in deep shock and badly concussed. Certainly won't be in any shape for us to talk to him for a couple of days."

"Well, well. Either this mysterious extortioner really does mean business or it was a most extraordinary coincidence," Otani said, and failed to notice a quick exchange of glances between his two subordinates. "I think I'll have a cigarette. You say your people are looking at the chandelier fitting, Hara?"

"Yes, sir. I'll have a report for you first thing in the morning."

"All I can say from a quick look myself," Kimura put in, "is that it had broken off at the central joint below the sort of inverted dome that houses the terminals. Where the wiring comes through from the ceiling. And that it looked corroded at the break. The sheer weight of the thing must have jerked the hooks securing the three safety chains clean out of the ceiling and wrenched the wiring out with it."

Hara was not to be outdone. "For your added information, sir, I have ascertained from Fire Brigade Headquarters that a routine safety inspection of the entire premises was carried out in July this year, and that the Tamahimeden management was complimented on its high standards."

Otani looked from one to the other. "Well, I suppose we mustn't jump to conclusions. Obviously it's absolutely right that the thing should be checked to see whether it had been interfered with, and if it has Uehara and his technical staff will have a few nasty questions to answer. Even if it was, though, it's hardly credible that it could have been *intended* that it should fall on Watanabe. It would have been impossible to predict exactly when it would collapse, surely. Anyway, we

63

shall see. I presume the party broke up at once, Kimura-kun?"

"Yes. I thought briefly of taking statements from people in the vicinity, but at the time the extent of Watanabe's injuries wasn't clear. On the whole it seemed better to minimise the fuss. After all, Uehara and Masako Yasuda were presumably the only people in the room apart from myself who knew anything about this fictitious extortioner and it would have looked odd if I'd started treating what looked like a complete accident as a police matter."

Hara coughed politely. "But if I may say so, it *is* a police matter," he said. "Thanks to Inspector Kimura, we now know that the so-called extortioner *is* fictitious. The man Kinjo must be extremely stupid. Not only can we be virtually certain that the postcode on the envelope containing the anonymous letter and the address on that containing the Inspector's invitation card were written by the same person, but we can identify the typewriter used."

Otani looked startled. "This is the first I've heard of it," he said tartly, and Kimura bit his lip in embarrassment.

"I realise that, sir, and I'm extremely sorry," he said. "The handwriting was suggestive, certainly, but insufficiently conclusive to report to you. And it was only this morning that I managed to get a specimen of typing from the Mode International office at the Tamahimeden. I sent Migishima over to ask Uehara for a copy of the invitation list for today's press conference, and Hara's been checking it today. He tells me it matches."

"I see. I'm glad you've seen fit to mention it now. So what you're telling me is that having set up with Kinjo's incompetent assistance what was otherwise a neat little trick to embezzle a lot of money, Masako Yasuda, or Uehara, or both, decided to call it off?"

"Er, yes, sir. In a manner of speaking."

"Then why go to the trouble of arranging a spectacular accident in the middle of their party?"

"That's what we need to find out, sir. Assuming that it

64

wasn't a genuine accident. If it was, a man like Watanabe will certainly expect a hefty solatium from the company who own the Tamahimeden. And if it wasn't, then it's a criminal matter. I can remember more or less who was nearby when the chandelier fell and might have seen more clearly than I did exactly how Uehara and the other two reacted, so I know who to ask for statements later on."

Slightly mollified, Otani nodded. "All right. Did you notice who called the ambulance?"

"I'm not sure. I was busy giving what I could in the way of first aid. Uehara or one of the Yasuda staff, I imagine. It would be easy enough to find out when we talk to the management in the morning. Practically everybody will be at the Tamahimeden, getting ready for the gala opening show the day after tomorrow."

Otani leant back, savouring his cigarette. With Hanae's patient and unobtrusive encouragement he had managed to cut his consumption to five or less a day but doubted if he would ever be able to do without them altogether. "In view of what's happened you'd better hold off challenging either Uehara or Kinjo about this bogus letter," he said. "Was he there this afternoon, by the way? Kinjo, I mean."

"Kinjo?" Kimura stared at his shoes in an effort to remember. "He was certainly at the press conference, but I don't think he stayed for the drinks party. I can't be absolutely sure, but I think I'd have remembered if he was."

Otani made a dismissive gesture. "It's probably of no importance," he said. "On the other hand this incident – and what you've told me this evening – means at the very least that we must keep a fairly close eye on these fashion people from now on until the whole thing's over. Somebody may or may not have intended harm to Watanabe. It's not inconceivable that. . ." His voice trailed away and he gazed absently at the ceiling before giving his head a little shake and resuming. "Never mind for now. Theorising's all very well, but what I need from you two are some positive suggestions about how to handle the next week or so. You've met some of the people it might be worth keeping in view, Kimura-kun, but you can hardly attach yourself to them for days on end."

In principle Kimura would have liked nothing better, but was realistic enough to remain silent.

Hara coughed deprecatingly. "As I reported to you earlier this evening, sir, when Inspector Kimura and I discussed this affair at an earlier stage I was perhaps unduly sceptical. Certainly I doubted whether anything would come of Mr Uehara's expressed forebodings, even when it was still in doubt whether they were genuine or assumed. It now seems more than possible that by tomorrow we shall have evidence of actual intent to disrupt the gathering at the Tamahimeden, and if not of intent to kill or injure, at the very least of a reckless disregard for the personal safety of those present. I have already assured Inspector Kimura of my readiness to cooperate with him in any way he thinks appropriate –"

"Yes, yes. Thank you. I agree that we must set this investigation up formally as of today, with the full involvement of your section, Inspector. I've been delighted to see how well you two work together, anyway. As you know, things were very different in your predecessor's time. . . well, the less said about Sakamoto the better, I suppose, poor fellow." Otani sighed heavily and without conscious thought lit another cigarette. The knowledge that former Inspector Sakamoto was languishing in a secure hospital for the criminally insane greatly troubled Otani, who still blamed himself for not having adopted a more sympathetic attitude towards him before his precarious mental equilibrium was hopelessly disturbed.

"Anyway, what I was about to say is that in order to avoid any possible crossing of lines I propose to take nominal charge. I should like you two to share operational responsibility, though. And I suppose we mustn't rule Ninja Noguchi out in view of his rather surprising knowledge of the background of this fellow, what was his name. . ."

"Kubota, chief." Kimura grinned ruefully. "I agree. It certainly doesn't sound like Ninja's department, but on past

66

form he's quite capable of producing the bent electrician who worked on that chandelier."

Hara looked a little shocked. "We should I feel wait for an authoritative technical report on the chandelier before making any assumption. . . I beg your pardon. I should have realised that Inspector Kimura is still exploring a mere hypothesis. If I may make a suggestion, sir?"

"By all means, Hara."

"Sir, I wonder if it might be possible to place a member of my section inconspicuously behind the scenes at the Tamahimeden. Senior Woman Detective Migishima is an officer of remarkable versatility and –"

"That's brilliant, Hara!" Hara blinked in confusion over the generosity of Kimura's tribute to him. "She could. . . let's see, what could she do?"

Hara recovered himself and went on. "It occurred to me that a fashion show must involve many rapid changes of costume, and that presumably female assistants are required to –"

"I suppose so," Otani said dubiously. "I really have no idea what goes on at these affairs."

"Hara's perfectly right," Kimura said. "And Junko-san could carry something like that off perfectly." Otani still brooded.

"I take your word for it, but I don't see how you could put her in place without this man Uehara knowing, and if he is in fact up to something, that would frustrate the whole object of the exercise."

A gloomy silence ensued, but the optimist in Kimura was rarely suppressed for long.

"I'm not so sure," he said after a while. "These designers may have favourite models, but they certainly don't cart a whole supporting staff of dressers around the world at enormous expense. And consider the regular business of the Tamahimeden – weddings. They must employ dressers there all the time to get the brides in and out of their various outfits. You know, formal bridal kimono first, then most of them

67

change into a white wedding dress half-way through the reception, and then into the going-away clothes. I'd be willing to bet that Uehara has arranged to use Tamahimeden staff, at least as helpers. If I'm right, we could sell the idea to the manager in confidence, especially if the chandelier business really was no accident. My guess is that he'll be only too glad to collaborate to help establish that his staff aren't at fault."

Otani stood up, Kimura and Hara hastily following suit. "Well, let's hope you're right. I leave it to you to sort out the tactics and we'd better meet here again tomorrow afternoon. I'm off home now. Thank you both for your invaluable advice. Goodnight."

The two inspectors bowed politely and Hara slipped unobtrusively out of the room first. Kimura was half-way through the door when Otani called him back. "By the way, Kimura, did you have a hand in this invitation my wife and I received from the Japan-British Society of the Kansai in Osaka for tomorrow evening?"

"What? Japan-British Society? No, absolutely not. I didn't even know about it."

Otani nodded gravely, his famous poker face proof against his amusement at Kimura's look of consternation. "Good. Then it must have been as my wife said. They asked us because of my being President of the Rokko Bonsai Club. According to the slip of paper enclosed with the invitation it's supposed to be in honour of the British participants in the Mode International show and these experts from Accrington."

"And are you going?" Kimura still looked dazed.

"Oh, I think we probably will," Otani said airily. "My wife's quite keen to." Kimura rightly interpreted this to mean that wild horses wouldn't keep Otani away. "Unless something urgent crops up. If you're not busy, why don't you organise yourself an invitation too? I'm sure you could fix it. I know you keep in touch with all these friendship societies, and it would be nice to see you there. You could always use the occasion to improve your acquaintance with the English model girl."

Chapter X

"Well, Gorgeous must have frightened the life out of the manager," Senior Woman Detective Junko Migishima said to her husband as she tucked her arm firmly under his and they set off for Sannomiya station to catch the bus home. It was just after six, and he had been hovering anxiously outside the Tamahimeden waiting for her for at least half an hour before she emerged and, to his inadequately disguised horror, kissed him enthusiastically.

Since Junko, at five feet three inches, was eight inches shorter and weighed only just over half as much as Migishima, this entailed her clambering up him rather as though attempting to climb a tree. Such a public display of physical affection would have been unheard of in the Japan of ten or fifteen years earlier and was still rare even among people of their generation, especially after three years of marriage. Junko adored her large, gentle husband, but thought it a very good thing to keep him up to date, especially as she now outranked him and knew that he often brooded about the fact. She also knew that he disapproved of her habit of referring to his own boss Kimura by a variety of disrespectful nicknames. "Gorgeous" was the flavour of the month, displacing "Pretty Boy" and "Fancy Pants" for the time being.

"What do you mean? Inspector Kimura told me when he came back to the office this morning that the manager had been only too pleased to collaborate by engaging you as a temporary assistant."

"I should say he was. There never was any doubt about that. The Professor briefed me with all his usual thoroughness, so I knew about the acid in the chandelier fitment and the loosened screws for the safety chains. I also knew the manager had been told that if he plays along it's very probable that the Tamahimeden management will be exonerated and won't have to pay Watanabe the huge compensation a man like that would be justified in demanding."

"Yes, I heard about that. I'm bound to say I don't see how we're in any position to guarantee that he won't. . ."

When Migishima worried he did so visibly, and Junko grinned up at him. "Tell you what, I don't feel like going straight home. Let's go and have something to eat, and I'll buy you a bottle of beer. Come on, we can afford *okonomiyaki*." She tugged at his hand, and after very little hesitation Migishima obediently set off in her wake.

"Anyway, the manager was so keen to cooperate that he introduced me to the wardrobe supervisor – she oversees the bridalwear rental department there too – as a niece of his from Fukuoka. Otherwise I suppose she'd have been put out, assuming she normally does the hiring for her department. I ask you, do I *sound* as if I come from Fukuoka?" Junko was in fact a local girl with a pleasant but perceptible Kansai accent, and Migishima shook his head even more dubiously. His wife indeed had a strong personality and extrovert ways, traits for which the women of the island of Kyushu are renowned, but she would have to watch her language if she was to pass muster among the other staff.

It was not until they were seated opposite each other in a

70

modest do-it-yourself restaurant and half-way through a bottle of Asahi beer that Junko's bubbling narrative of the day's events had so seized his imagination that he had cheered up. "So you can see that although I was fed up when the Professor told me to drop the Church of Divine Posession caper for the time being, this Mode International assignment has its compensations," Junko said as she brushed a little oil on the gas-heated griddle built into the table between them to fry the bits and pieces of chopped raw vegetables and shreds of pork from the bowl the waitress had brought, dousing them with soy sauce when they began to sizzle.

"Is Inspector Hara going to put somebody else on the case?"

Junko shook her head decisively as she turned the cooking meat and vegetables over expertly with the flat metal spreader provided, flattened the pile and dumped a heap of bean sprouts on top. "He'd better not. I want Brother Yamanaka all for myself." The bean sprouts soon softened, and Junko once again pressed everything down. Migishima swallowed in anticipation as she emptied a bowl of batter over the lot and their cheap but filling meal began to take its final shape.

For the past month Junko had been looking into the activities of the founder and patriarch of a new religious sect based in the castle town of Himeji to the west of Kobe. She had as yet formed no final view about the divinity or otherwise of the so-called church whose services she had been attending on weekday afternoons in the company of a surprisingly large number of other married women of all ages in Brother Yamanaka's large, isolated house, but she believed she had amassed almost enough evidence to satisfy the district prosecutor that the undoubtedly charming founder certainly believed in gaining possession of the cash savings of his disciples, and in the case of the younger and more attractive among them, their persons also. Money which Japanese wives set aside for a rainy day is known as "belly-button money" since the traditional place of concealment was the

71

voluminous *obi* sash worn with the kimono, and the founder was obviously very good at uncovering it.

"Help yourself." The huge, plumply stuffed pancake had been turned over, and Junko divided it unevenly with the spreader, taking only a third of it herself but attacking her share vigorously with a pair of the throwaway chopsticks from the bamboo container beside the soy-sauce bottle. "Anyway," she resumed after two or three hearty mouthfuls and a sip of beer, "I did what I was told by the other girls and got on with them pretty well. At first it was mainly a question of unpacking and ironing, fetching and carrying, but there was a full-scale rehearsal this afternoon for the gala preview tomorrow, and I soon got roped into helping the models in and out of the clothes. It was absolute chaos at the Tamahimeden today, of course. Heaven knows what the Yasuda organisation are paying for the exclusive use of the place for a whole week. It's still crawling with workmen – they've built a stage and catwalk in the biggest reception room and they're still tinkering with a very fancy lighting and sound system they've installed. It must have been the easiest thing in the world during the last couple of days for one of them to fix that chandelier. People are wandering about with ladders all over the place."

Migishima interrupted the methodical demolition of his meal. "You were beginning to tell me about the foreign models," he said. "Inspector Kimura thought there were just two of them, the rest Japanese."

"No. The English and the American girls are what you might call the stars, brought here specially by two of the designers. Somebody said Masako Yasuda tried to get Marie Helvin to come, but she turned her down flat. Of course, if it had been Kansai Yamamoto who'd asked her it might have been different – he discovered her in the first place." Migishima goggled at her uncomprehendingly. He had no idea who Marie Helvin might be, or Kansai Yamamoto for that matter.

Junko smiled pityingly. "Marie Helvin is half Japanese,

and she and Jerry Hall are about the most famous models in the world. And Kansai Yamamoto is the designer who gave her the big break by taking her to London when she was very young. But don't try to remember, because neither of them are here now. Two very well-known foreign models are, plus another four gaijin who work the Tokyo circuit regularly, and eight Japanese, including one young man. I should have realised that they need a couple of male models as well as the girls. I met most of them today during their rehearsal breaks. One of the foreigners is a man, too. You've seen him on TV. He does the commercials for Black Nikka whisky. He's an American, with a Japanese wife, lives in Tokyo permanently. Then there's a really nice Swedish girl called Erika who speaks perfect Japanese, I was talking to her at lunchtime and she told me about the others. Her parents were missionaries and she grew up here. She said foreigners all laugh when they hear there's a brand of whisky called Black Nikka."

Migishima pondered, but although his own command of English was improving rapidly, finally shook his head, baffled. Not much of a whisky drinker himself, he rather preferred Black Nikka to the more popular Suntory Old, and failed to see anything funny about it. "And she lives in Tokyo as well?" He began to make a gesture of refusal as Junko signalled to the waitress for another bottle of beer, but then thought better of it and ate another lump of pancake instead.

"No. She left with her parents when she was seventeen. She was telling me about the system for foreign models in Japan. It's fascinating. They can stay for up to two months with a working visa, then go out of the country to Korea, Guam or Hong Kong and come back for another two months. At the end of that time they can do the same thing once more, but after that they have to take a six-month break before coming back to Japan. That's when they mostly go to work in Europe. It's all legal and above-board, not like the strippers and call-girls who come in on tourist visas and take a chance. They pay twenty per cent tax on what's left after the agent's commission."

"There can't be very many of them, surely?"

73

"More than you'd think. Erika said there are two big agencies called Folio and SOS in Tokyo with about sixty foreign models each on their books, but she's with Image. Apparently it's the most exclusive – only half a dozen girls – and charges the highest fees."

Migishima nodded sagely and fell silent. Junko could almost hear him thinking, and smiled sweetly at him. "No, I don't think they are," she said as he eventually opened his mouth to speak again.

"You don't think they're what?"

"Jealous of the English and American girls who were brought in specially. That is what you were going to ask, isn't it?" Junko remorsefully reached out for her husband's hand as she saw the woebegone look on his face. "I'm sorry. I shouldn't put words into your mouth, but the same thought occurred to me. That either Erika or Gene – that's the American from Tokyo – resented the publicity Vanessa and Barbi are getting and wanted to spoil the drinks party for them. Or any of the other models who weren't invited to it. It really is a pretty wild idea, you know, even if one of them could have got into that room and damaged the chandelier. Gene seems to be such a pleasant, easy-going man, and Erika and the other foreign girls are just too nice to react like that, I'm quite certain."

"Why do you call them all by their first names?" Migishima enquired, not completely mollified. He accepted without hesitation Junko's intuitive assessment of the characters of the foreigners and consequent rejection of what had in any case been an absurdly far-fetched hypothesis. He was, on the other hand, rather taken aback by the informal way in which she referred to her new acquaintances. Privately relieved that Junko was, even if only temporarily, out of the potential clutches of the sinister Brother Yamanaka and his highly personal interpretation of the notion of Divine Possession, he wasn't altogether happy about her approving reference to Gene.

Junko shrugged. "Everybody's on first-name terms, even

74

the Japanese," she said. "It's like the theatre. When people spend a lot of their working lives undressing in front of each other I should think they'd find it rather silly to call each other Mr Hashimoto or Miss Radley."

Migishima sat up straight, his high colour not entirely due to the effect of more than his fair share of the two bottles of beer. "Yes," he said manfully, "I suppose so. All the same, surely Inspector Hara suggested that you should concentrate on finding out as much as you can from the Japanese models rather than bothering with foreigners? They're much more likely to gossip about Madame Yasuda and Uehara, even perhaps Watanabe."

"Of course. I talked to them a bit too, but they didn't have much time. Gorgeous's girl friend was interviewing them during their rest periods. You know, that superior Kyoto person slumming it on the *Kobe Shimbun*. I say, do you think he's enrolled *her* in the investigation? It would be like his cheek."

"I don't think you're quite fair about Nakazato-san," Migishima protested, doggedly reasonable as always. Having over a long period had to field many phone calls from women of a variety of nationalities wanting to speak to Kimura, he was rather hoping that his current single-minded pursuit of the elegant young lady with the quizzical look in her eye would result in marriage and relative peace and quiet in the office. "She's earning her own living like us, and she can't help it if she comes from a privileged background. To answer your question, I very much doubt it. I'm sure the inspector wouldn't have discussed confidential police business with her. She does work on the women's page of the paper, after all, and these Mode International shows are a very big thing for the local media."

"Oh, well. You may be right, but I have my doubts. I suppose we ought to be going," Junko said, delving into her bag and handing over a thousand-yen note. "This is for the beer."

"Thank you," Migishima said politely. They often ate out after work when they happened to be rostered for duty together, and scrupulously took it in turn to pay for the food.

"Anyway, I didn't find out anything interesting from the Japanese girls," Junko said cheerfully as they left the restaurant and headed for the nearest bus stop. "I can tell you one thing, though, Uehara was going about looking ghastly. You'd have thought the chandelier had fallen on him rather than Watanabe."

Chapter XI

Although she usually enjoyed a little sake with her evening meal, Hanae had never been really tipsy in her life, but half-way through the Japan-British Society reception at the Osaka Royal Hotel she realised with surprise that she was nearer to that state than ever before. She had seldom even tasted spirits, except on the rare occasions when her husband was either very excited or under great pressure and took it into his head to press on her some of the whisky which normally reposed in a kitchen cupboard undisturbed for months on end. Now, clutching a glass containing the remains of her third gin and tonic and having for the past few minutes been hearing her own voice as though it belonged to somebody else, she reluctantly decided that enough was enough and declined a passing waiter's offer of a replacement with a polite, slightly lopsided smile.

"That's your husband over there, isn't it? Talking to those English people?"

Hanae nodded with pride. She was having a lovely time.

Not only did she think her Tetsuo looked quite splendid in his best dark suit with the tie they had presented to him at Cambridge University, but she was well satisfied with her own appearance. The maple-leaf viewing season was upon them, and had more or less dictated her choice of the predominantly russet-coloured kimono which was one of her favourites and was still entirely suitable for a woman of her age. Hanae was resolved to be sensible about the advancing years, but attitudes were changing and these days there was no need for a woman to go into the drab colours of old age while still in her early fifties. It was nice that she had her old acquaintance Mrs Ebihara to talk to, and not altogether displeasing to see that she was wearing a rather strange Western-style cocktail dress which exposed her prominent collarbones and a scrawny expanse of bosom, and probably accounted for the un-characteristic timidity of her smile. With so many well-to-do British ladies about Mrs Ebihara would have done much better to stick to the traditional Japanese dress that she usually wore with some panache.

"Yes, he's with the delegation of bonsai experts from Lancashire Prefecture. The Consul General particularly wanted them to meet him. I think I may have mentioned that he's president of the Rokko Bonsai Club."

"Yes, you did," Mrs Ebihara said. "I would have liked to introduce my son-in-law to you both. He frequently comes down from Tokyo of course and I had hoped he would join us this evening, but my daughter rang to say he can't get away from the studios today after all. He's not reading the news tonight but has to chair an important discussion about the future of education."

"Good evening, Mrs Otani. The Superintendent seems to be in demand." It was Kimura, and Hanae rewarded him with a particularly warm smile. She was quite ready to detach herself from Mrs Ebihara now that the conversation had taken the inevitable turn. "He's explaining the finer points of the dwarf pine to the visitors. The assistant secretary of the Japan-British Society is doing a fine job of interpreting."

Hanae smiled again, rather wishing Kimura hadn't mentioned the interpreter. Sooner or later Mrs Ebihara would be bound to express well-bred surprise at the fact that Otani spoke no English.

"This is Inspector Kimura, a close colleague of my husband," she said. "My friend Mrs Ebihara." By the time they had finished bowing to each other Hanae was determined to escape. "Shall we join them, Mr Kimura? Mrs Ebihara, you will excuse our bad manners, I know."

As they made their way circuitously to the dais by the microphone Hanae suddenly giggled uncontrollably, then blushed and raised her free hand to conceal her mouth. The bonsai under examination was in an unglazed brown ceramic bowl on a brocade-covered table on the dais, backed by a plain gold folding screen, and was indeed a handsome specimen. Kimura stopped and looked at Hanae in amused surprise, and she felt she owed him an explanation.

"I'm so sorry," she said, suppressing the giggles only with great difficulty. "It's just that the bonsai with the screen behind it looks like the back of a Noh play stage, and my husband. . ." She broke down again and Kimura chuckled with her as he saw the point. Some fifteen yards away from them Otani was obviously holding forth at some length to his new friends from Accrington, and no doubt to make his meaning clearer had assumed a peculiar attitude with one hand raised in the air and the other held stiffly across his body. He remained frozen in this stance as the young lady at his side interpreted for him, and even in his smart Western-style suit the effect he created as seen from a distance was indeed uncannily like that of a tense moment in a Noh play.

Kimura and Hanae remained where they were for a minute or two longer, and almost but not quite unconsciously she accepted another gin and tonic and sipped at it as she willingly allowed Kimura to practise his charm on her. Listening to him prattling on amusingly and with an air of great, if bogus, authority about the fashion business as he pointed out Wesley Wilberforce, Terry Phipps and Vanessa Radley to her, Hanae could see perfectly well why her husband frequently arrived home in a state of exasperation about his bumptiousness. Nevertheless, he *was* undoubtedly a very attractive man, and she greatly preferred his company to that of Mrs Ebihara. All the same, Hanae kept half an eye on the earnest bonsai seminar, and after a while she intercepted a discreet signal from Otani.

"I think my husband wants me, Mr Kimura," she said with some regret. "I've so much enjoyed talking to you. I would have been very nervous otherwise at a grand affair like this. I suppose somebody like you would find it hard to believe that from the time I was married until my daughter was grown up I never once went out in the evening?" Hanae spoke no more than the simple truth, and the same could be said of the overwhelming majority of respectable women of her generation.

Kimura watched her until she had joined her husband and was bowing to the Lancastrians, and was visited by a brief vision of Mie Nakazato in a similar situation in perhaps ten years' time. Like the handful of the most senior officers in every prefectural police force, Kimura was a government official, an officer of the National Police Agency and not an employee of the local authority. If and when the time came for him to be appointed to the command of a prefectural force it could be anywhere in the country, but would almost certainly not be Hyogo. He sighed. Mie was an extremely attractive girl who clearly liked him, but had, in spite of the sensuality of her kisses, for months remained immune to his attempts to seduce her. Ever wary, he assumed that she had marriage in mind, and in his more introspective moments wondered whether he was himself weakening; whether he had in fact tried very hard to get her into bed and if not, why not.

"Gosh, what an old fiddle-face!" cried Sara Byers-Pinkerton, appearing abruptly at his side in a cream silk Chinese embroidered blouse and black satin trousers. "What's up, somebody pinched your drink? Have to keep your beady eyes on this lot, you know." She turned to her companions. "This is *him*, Duggie," she added delightedly. "The sexy detective from my past. Haven't seen him for ages and now he keeps popping up everywhere I go. Looking all noble and suffering like that because you're here, shouldn't wonder."

Remembering the wedding photograph he had seen on the mantelpiece on the occasion of his one and only visit to the Byers-Pinkerton residence in Kobe, Kimura could just about discern the face of the young bridegroom with the cruelly brushed hair and neat moustache in the plumply pink features of the balding middle-aged man who must be her husband. In her party clothes and properly made-up, Mrs B-P on the other hand looked surprisingly appetising, if not in the same league as Selena Stoke-Lacy in asymmetrical layers of sage-green linen and Vanessa Radley, towering over her aristocratically, half in and half out of a blood-red silk satin sheath slit to the thigh.

"Good evening, ladies. Good evening, Mr Byers-Pinkerton. Kimura's my name. Miss Radley, a pleasure to meet you."

"Oh. Ah. Heard quite a bit about you. How d'you do." Seemingly unmoved by his wife's remarks, Douglas Byers-Pinkerton first viewed Kimura with a look of bland complacency on his face and then extended a hand affably enough.

"Ere, din I see yer yessdy? When the lights fell on that ole bloke's 'ead? Mussen arf've 'urt but I at ta laugh." It took all Kimura's self-control to prevent himself from gasping in astonishment at the weird sounds which issued from Vanessa Radley's exquisitely chiselled lips.

"Yes, indeed you did, Tracy," Selena said. "The inspector seems to be keeping a careful eye on all of us."

With something of an effort, Kimura regained his presence of mind and shrugged. "Pure coincidence, I assure you. As a matter of fact I'm here on account of the bonsai experts from England, not Mode International. My boss is the president of one of the local clubs and I came along with him to lend a hand with interpreting, but it turned out he didn't need me –"

"Tracy my sweet, Her Ladyship wants you and you know how she sulks if she's kept waiting – oh, hullo, it's you again is it? Oh, blissful, darling. Do it *just* like that for the photographers and pop it in your composite, but come on, do, or we shall have a *volcanically* agitated frockist on our hands." Vanessa Radley continued to pout most beautifully but nevertheless allowed Terry Phipps to tow her away.

"What an extraordinary little man. 'Pop it in her composite'? Sounds jolly rude to me," Mrs B-P said in a bewildered tone as her husband gazed at Terry's retreating back with acute distaste written all over his face. Selena, on the other hand, was smiling for the first time that Kimura had noticed, though he observed also that it was with her lips only. The grey-green eyes remained cold.

"Terry's rather sweet, really," she said. "A composite's just a model's portfolio of favourite photos, that's all. Combined with a 'good book' or record of work it's what her agency needs to keep her at the top for another few months until people want a different sort of face."

"All right, swank-pot, no need to show off in front of this gorgeous man." Mrs B-P put out her tongue at her cousin and then winked ostentatiously at Kimura, who, for all his cosmopolitan savoir-faire, found himself acutely embarrassed.

Douglas Byers-Pinkerton cleared his throat thunderously, having appeared to come to a decision. "Time we were off if we're going to look in at the Volpicellis' party, Crumbles," he announced. "And we ought to. You coming with us after all, Selena?"

As Selena shook her head Mrs B-P groaned theatrically. "Beast! Tyrant! Sadist!" she went on to state loudly and clearly as those of her acquaintances within earshot glanced at her with tolerant smiles and strangers pretended not to hear. Then she turned to Kimura and assumed a penetrating stage whisper. "I told you so. *Consumed* with jealousy. I shall probably be beaten within an inch of my life when we get home." She rolled her eyes, clutched at her breast and then blew a kiss at him before turning to her husband and resuming her normal tones. "All right then, you mean old sod," she said cheerfully. "We'll totter off to your ghastly Italians and leave these children to enjoy themselves."

Kimura was concious of a burgeoning respect for Douglas Byers-Pinkerton, who not only appeared to remain unperturbed by his wife's extravagant speech and behaviour but again shook his hand cordially. "Enjoyed talking to you, Inspector," he said. "Drop in at the house some time. Drink or two. Got your map for the taxi-driver, Selena? Right then. See you later."

"I shan't be all that late, but don't wait up. And don't say it, Sara," Selena added warningly, and Mrs B-P obediently put a finger across her lips. Slightly battered by the encounter and temporarily bereft of words, Kimura bowed in farewell to her. Then they were gone, though Mrs B-P's ringing tones continued to be audible for some time as she apologised profusely and insincerely to the people they bumped into on their way to the doors.

"She often affects people like that."

"I beg your pardon?" Kimura closed his mouth and pulled himself together as he realised with some surprise that Selena Stoke-Lacy was still at his side and showed no particular inclination to escape.

"I mean, Sara can be a bit overpowering if you don't know her all that well."

"Yes. I suppose so." Kimura's professional curiosity began to revive. "What was it you didn't want her to say?"

Selena raised her eyes heavenward. "When she's embarrassed my cousin tends to fall back on clichés. She was quite certainly about to tell me not to do anything she wouldn't do, and possibly also to tell me that if I can't be good I should be careful."

Kimura wasn't quite sure that he followed Selena's drift, and seized on the one clear impression which her cousin's exit had left with him. "She didn't seem very embarrassed to me," he said.

"Oh, but she was, I assure you. I wouldn't tell her why I wanted to talk to you, you see, so she jumped to conclusions."

"You want to talk to me?" Kimura beamed expansively, being constitutionally incapable of any other reaction when sought out by an attractive woman.

There was no answering warmth in Selena's face. "I said Sara jumped to conclusions when I asked her to bring us over and get into conversation with you. There's no need for you to do the same. Obviously I had no idea you would turn up here, but I'm glad you did. As soon as I spotted you I made up a vague excuse about going off to dinner with Wesley, Terry and Tracy afterwards. To get out of going with Sara and Doug."

"I see," said Kimura, who didn't. "Well, if there's something I can do for you. . .?"

"I don't want people to see us go out together. Is there somewhere you could meet me in half an hour's time?"

He stood very still for a moment before replying. "It's something important, then? I see. All right, listen carefully. It's not all that cold this evening. Go out of the main entrance of this hotel, turn right and walk straight along the main road with the canal on your left for about five minutes. You'll see the Osaka Festival Hall with a big sign in English facing you to your right, and the Osaka Grand Hotel on the canal front adjoining it. I'll wait for you in the Pine Bar in the basement to the left of the main lobby as you go in. Got that?"

"Turn right, look for the Osaka Festival Hall, Pine Bar in basement of Osaka Grand Hotel adjoining. Yes. Thank you." Selena flashed him a brilliant social smile and slipped away to join the little knot of people gathered round Wesley Wilberforce.

It was not easy for Kimura to make his farewells to the Otanis. Pink-cheeked and vivacious, Hanae seemed delighted to see him again and more than ready to embark on

84

another conversation. The Consul General, it seemed, had introduced her to the famous Mr Wesley Wilberforce who had been absolutely charming, been fascinated to hear about her daughter and son-in-law in London, and ended up by inviting her to the Mode International gala preview the next day. Otani presumably knew nothing of this, since he was nodding his head sagaciously over a pile of photographs being shown to him by a particularly tall and thin Accrington bonsai fancier who wore a cardigan under the jacket of his suit. The young lady interpreting for him wore a fixed, desperate smile, and dabbed at her forehead with a tiny handkerchief as Kimura butted in to excuse himself.

By the time Kimura reached the doors there was no sign of Selena Stoke-Lacy, but he spotted her walking fast with her head down when he was about half-way to the other hotel, and soon caught up with her. He called her name while still some yards behind her and saw her freeze momentarily before relaxing and turning to meet him.

"Thank you for coming," she said. "I should probably apologise. Maybe you have a date or something."

"No. It's fine. Shall we go into the Grand Hotel or would you prefer to walk and talk? Oh, I'm sorry. Are you cold?"

"No. That isn't why I was shivering. Let's stay here. Look at the canal or something."

Kimura shrugged. "Osaka used to be called the Venice of the East, but not any more. Not with the pollution, and the motorways built on stilts over the canals. It's easy to forget we're on a little island here, especially at this time of the year when the water doesn't smell too bad."

He led the way across the road and they stood by the parapet looking down at the sullen black waters of the canal which mirrored the neon signs on the buildings opposite. "How is that man who was hit by the chandelier?" Selena asked abruptly.

"Not too bad, I believe. He's getting on in years but pretty tough, it seems. But that's not what you wanted to talk to me about, is it?"

The woman at his side gave a deep, shuddering sigh. "In a way," she said. "You see, I think somebody's trying to kill Stom."

"Stom?"

"Kubota. Tsutomu Kubota. I – we call him Stom."

The next forty-five minutes proved to be both interesting and maddeningly frustrating for Kimura. It was as though having given voice to her fears Selena deeply regretted having done so, and she seemed able or willing to tell Kimura very little more. She turned down his suggestion that they should go somewhere to eat, and insisted on going back to Kobe by the interurban train even though he offered to splurge on a taxi. On the way she seemed to take refuge in talking about herself, explaining how in order to complete her degree in modern languages she had spent a year as an assistant in a school in Rouen. Two years experience as a secretary at the Paris office of the *International Herald-Tribune* commended her to the editor of a local newspaper in Kent, and Kimura gathered that her talents as a journalist soon flowered to the point at which she was able to leap the hurdle into Fleet Street.

Paris-based Tsutomu Kubota had, it seemed, been one of her subjects in a series of articles about "Les Enfants Terribles" of the world of fashion design, and her command of French the key which had unlocked the door to his confidence. Selena's account of their ripening acquaintance was both allusive and disjointed, but as he listened Kimura became certain that they must soon have become lovers. He tried to elicit from her some idea when all this had happened, but without success. Selena would not answer direct questions. She volunteered what she chose to, and otherwise simply remained silent. By the time they reached Sannomiya in central Kobe and began the ten-minute walk to the Byers-Pinkerton house, he was still unable to judge whether her affair with Kubota had ended several years previously or whether it was still going on.

"Look," he said finally in some desperation as they turned the corner by a sake shop he remembered from last time and saw the kindergarten almost opposite the high wall which concealed all but the uppermost part of the eccentric English couple's spacious house. "You asked for this conversation. You began it by telling me that you think somebody may be trying to kill Kubota-san. But you still haven't told me why you think so, you haven't told me who you think might want to or for what reason, and you haven't told me what in the world you expect me to do about it. You must see what an impossible position you're putting me in."

They had arrived at the Byers-Pinkertons' gate, and he stared sternly at the pale face illuminated by the lamp above it. Apart from themselves the street was deserted, the silence not so much broken as underlined by the plaintive, unearthly beauty of the sound of somebody practising the bamboo flute in a nearby house.

"I know. I'm sorry. I – it's just so difficult to. . ." Selena hesitated yet again, but seemed to be nerving herself to come to the point at last. Then to Kimura's utter astonishment she suddenly flung her arms around his neck.

It was as embarrassing as it was unexpected, because he heard a car turning into the street and even in a Japan notably more relaxed about public displays of affection than it had been even ten years earlier it was simply not done for people of mature years to embrace in the street. Instinctively he tried to free himself, but Selena tightened her grasp. "Kiss me, damn you!" she whispered urgently, and finally managed to clamp her mouth on his as the car drew up a few yards beyond them at the entrance to the garage at the side of the house and Kimura heard the doors being opened.

"I *say*! I warned you he was hot stuff, Selena. Didn't expect you to try him for yourself quite so soon, though."

Kimura's own confusion as Sara Byers-Pinkerton came and peered at them was unfeigned, but he retained enough presence of mind to notice how neatly Selena disengaged herself and assumed the wry look of somebody caught in the act, but not all that displeased by the situation.

"Trust you to turn up just at that moment," she said coolly. In the background her cousin's husband could be heard busily opening the garage doors in order to put the car away. "Jiro was just leaving. You nearly missed it. Goodnight, Jiro. See you again soon."

Chapter XII

As unobtrusively as she could, Hanae slipped into a chair
several rows back from the catwalk which had been erected in
the largest and most exuberantly decorated reception room at
the Tamahimeden wedding hall, hoping that Mrs Ebihara
would not turn up there too. The stage backed with a ceiling-
high screen was just to her left, and high on the wall facing it at
the other end of the room was a lighting engineer's box
supported by undisguised scaffolding painted in silver and
black. Lights and speakers jutted at odd angles from two
ceiling-mounted rails which ran for almost the full length of
the room, giving it, for all its rococo decor, something of the
look of a television studio. It would be bound to remind Mrs
Ebihara of her son-in-law's working environment, and Hanae
didn't think she could cope with her again so soon.

On balance, she rather regretted having come at all. A wan
little smile flickered at the corner of her mouth as she recalled
her husband's pleasure and surprise at her wantonly amorous
behaviour with him the previous evening when they had

arrived home, but there was no escaping the fact that she had been, not to put too fine a point upon it, drunk. At three-twenty in the afternoon she still had a queasy stomach and the troublesome remains of a headache to remind her. What was worse, Otani's enthusiastic response to her demands and his general mood of gratification over the respectful friendliness of the people from Accrington, and their reaction when he had asked about their local football team, had not survived breakfast, during which Hanae had mentioned her invitation to the gala preview and intention to be present.

Hanae had no idea why her husband had seemed so put out at the idea of her going, especially in view of his earlier naïve suggestion that she should save enough from the house-keeping money to buy herself a dress from the collection. She knew of course about Masako Yasuda's lucrative business arrangement with her former lover Watanabe and had noticed a paragraph in the previous morning's *Kobe Shimbun* to the effect that the president of the Wakamatsu company had met with an unfortunate accident at a party following the Mode International press conference and required medical treatment. The paper had made it sound as though he had been involved in a brawl of some kind.

However, Hanae knew nothing of any real or fictitious extortioner's demands, nor that Watanabe had within the past few hours been moved to the intensive care unit at the Kaigan Hospital just a few hundred metres away from the glamour and glitter of the Tamahimeden.

She shifted uneasily in her seat, wondering whether at this stage it would be too absurd to slip out and go quietly home, then told herself not to be so feeble. Although even when in her normal state of complete sobriety she understood scarcely more English than Otani, Hanae had no doubt that Wesley Wilberforce had made a great fuss of her when the Japanese chairman of the Japan-British Society of the Kansai had introduced her as the wife of the commander of the Hyogo prefectural police force. It was with pride that she had shown Otani, as he tackled his toast and marmalade, the handsomely embossed invitation card which Wilberforce had taken from the little stack Terry Phipps produced like a conjurer from his neat handbag, scribbled on and then pressed upon her, insistent that she should see the show; and her husband's reaction had been both inexplicable and hurtful. Old-fashioned middle-class housewife Hanae might be, but she had never lacked spirit. Her head throbbing, she had therefore told her husband quietly but firmly that she might not have arrived back from the preview by the time he got home and that if she was not there he would have to run his own bath. Now, sitting there in the rapidly filling room, she took a deep breath and decided that this was no time to let either herself or Mr Wilberforce down.

Determined but still disconsolate, Hanae surveyed the animated scene, surmising that there was probably room for about two hundred spectators and wondering how many of them had in fact paid fifteen thousand yen, the price of a night in a good hotel room, for their seats. Not the many ladies and three gentlemen of the Consular Corps greeting each other effusively as they took their designated front-row seats, certainly. Not the prefectural governor's wife, nor the people armed with note-books whom she took to be fashion writers. And surely not. . . it couldn't be. . . but it definitely *was* Inspector Hara, his glasses flashing as he sidled awkwardly into a seat in the back row behind her and a good distance away to her right, near the extreme end of the catwalk.

Hanae hastily buried herself in the glossy programme she had been given, and tried to concentrate on a biographical note about Jean-Claud Villon. She had only actually met Hara once, when he was in uniform, and had seen him from a distance on one other occasion as he was going into the zoo with his pregnant wife, his little daughter and, most unexpectedly, Ninja Noguchi. That day, of course, he had been in casual clothes. Even so, there was no doubt in her mind that the tall, moon-faced man in the dark suit who looked like a university teacher was the new senior member of her husband's staff. It was all most peculiar. Hanae would not

91

have been in the least surprised to meet Kimura there and it would indeed have cheered her up to do so, but he was nowhere to be seen. Instead the head of the criminal investigation section was – she peeped furtively behind her – sitting stiffly in the middle of a gaggle of women who obviously knew each other, and staring fixedly at the catwalk as the main doors of the improvised theatre were closed and the babble of conversation began to subside.

Hanae had never before been to a fashion show, and her ideas about the form they took had been shaped decades earlier when she had gazed enthralled in the cinema at the newsreels showing a succession of haughty young ladies mincing a few steps, turning, removing a coat or unbuttoning the jacket of a two-piece, and then withdrawing to make way for the next. Television and pictures in women's magazines had left her with a vague impression that things had changed a good deal since her young days, but she was nevertheless quite unprepared for what happened after the lights were first dimmed and then, a second or two later, extinguished altogether.

At once her ears were assailed from all sides by sliding, shifting waves of synthesised sound which imperceptibly resolved themselves into a surreal fanfare as one by one the letters spelling out MODE INTERNATIONAL blazed out in rainbow colours above the stage, pulsed eerily in time with the unearthly music, then changed to a uniform dusty gold as the fanfare shuddered to a climax and a spotlight lanced down to the diminutive figure of Kuniko Doi, centre stage. She was wearing a kind of Mao suit, also in gold, and her face was made up somewhat like that of a geisha, a tiny brilliant red cupid's-bow mouth like a wound against the dead white of her cheeks. The close-cropped hair familiar to tens of millions of viewers all over Japan went with the bizarre make-up surprisingly effectively.

"Ladies and gentlemen! Welcome to Mode International! *Minasama! Yoku irasshaimashita!*" The sound reproduction system was superb, and the husky voice caressed Hanae's ears as intimately as it did on those afternoons when she succumbed to the temptation to tune in to the deliciously outrageous "Kuniko's Friends" programme. Even hearing her speak alternately in English and Japanese wasn't all that strange, because from time to time Kuniko Doi welcomed foreign women guests to her show, and when this happened she invariably took the opportunity to essay a few sentences in English before reverting to Japanese in order to deploy her renowned *doubles entendres*.

These were very much in evidence and delighted her audience as the show began in earnest and she introduced each part, devoted to the work of one designer, withdrawing during the performance to a kind of throne placed for her to one side of the stage. Comment was impossible during each sequence as pop music blared out deafeningly, multi-coloured laser beams criss-crossed the room, strobe lights jarred the eye and the models emerged from behind the screen, pranced and cavorted in twos and threes, gestured, embraced and flung themselves and their partners into seemingly impossible attitudes before freezing sculpturally until released by applause.

The whole thing was wittily choreographed, slickly produced and stunningly effective, and Hanae thought she would have enjoyed it enormously if only the noise hadn't made her headache much worse and the strobe lights made the queasiness in her stomach intensify to the point of near-nausea. It was such a pity, because Hanae liked most of the clothes very much. Wesley Wilberforce's cottons were on the whole safe and pretty, Marian Norton's silk jerseys clinging and dramatic, Tsutomu Kubota's loosely-stitched canvas panels boldly angular and strange, and Jean-Claud Villon's frothy chiffons and gauzes teasingly sexy. Naturally enough Masako Yasuda's own creations were shown last of all, the one-offs brilliantly conceived, as always, to loosen the purse-strings of wealthy but not-so-young Tokyo women, while those intended for wider sale to their provincial sisters and their daughters seemed certain to keep cash-registers in her Wakamatsu boutiques busy.

93

Hanae in fact saw only the very beginning of the final sequence, because all at once a cold sweat broke out on her forehead, a sour metallic taste rose up into her throat and she knew that her stomach was about to revolt. It was desperately embarrassing to have to stumble past the other spectators in her row to reach the gap at the end of her block and make for the nearest door, but the consequences of not doing so would have been unimaginably worse.

She felt a little better immediately in the relative coolness of the wider corridor, and better still when a wild look round revealed a ladies' room a few yards along on the opposite side and she flung herself inside just in time.

Five minutes later Hanae emerged deathly pale and trembling slightly, but feeling much relieved and almost herself again. It was clearly out of the question for her to go back for the remainder of the show, though, and she thought she might as well slip out of the building altogether, thus avoiding any possible chance of meeting Inspector Hara face to face. On the other hand it would be very nice to sit somewhere quietly for a few minutes to recover her equanimity before venturing out into the cold. Although muffled, the orgiastic fortissimo of the music was all too audible where she hesitated indecisively, and Hanae retreated from it into a smaller connecting corridor.

Lushly carpeted like the rest of the building, it looked very like a hotel corridor with doors on either side every few yards, but little white plastic signs with black lettering indicated that behind the doors were changing-rooms for the use of the brides and grooms who normally populated the Tama-himeden. It was not a case of over-provision; Hanae could well believe that on the specially propitious days which fall four or five times every month and are indicated on every Japanese calendar there could well be a dozen or more wedding receptions going on in the building, many of them overlapping. Cards had been affixed to some of the doors and Hanae recognised one or two of the names on them as being those of visiting designers. The idea of taking temporary refuge in one of the rooms was clearly impracticable, and with a small sigh Hanae headed towards the green illuminated EXIT sign at the other end.

One only of the doors was ajar, and Hanae paused as she was about to pass it. There was obviously not a soul about, and since the programme had indicated that all the designers would be introduced at the end of the show it seemed safe to assume that they would all be backstage by then. Not since her daugher Akiko's wedding eight years before had Hanae been inside such a room, and she was curious to see just how luxurious the much-vaunted facilities of the Tamahimeden were.

She therefore coughed and then, since there was still no sound whatever from within, pushed the door open a few inches further and peeped timidly round it.

It had been one of the most hectic days in Junko Migishima's life, and she had neither heard nor seen anything apart from the distraught look on Hiroshi Uehara's face which seemed to her to relate in any way to the investigation in which she was supposed to be involved. Nevertheless, she was revelling in the controlled chaos of the changing-room adjoining the main salon before and during the show, and being a girl of high intelligence and great dexterity had soon made herself indispensable. Her fingers were sore and aching from fastening and unfastening hooks and zips, and there were several even more exhausting days to come with three shows each for the general public. Even the gala preview day wasn't over yet, but with all the models now on stage for the finale and the designers taking their bows, there was at least a moment for her to make a quick dash to the ladies' room.

Junko was on her way cheerfully back to the fray when she heard the unmistakable gulps, whimpers and wobbling, tentative wailing of a hysterical woman coming from the side corridor. She hesitated for no more than a moment, then turned and headed for the source of the unnerving noise.

Hanae was in no state of mind to recognise the young

woman in the pale blue smock overall who entered the room after knocking sharply and calling out a brisk "Excuse me!" She continued to stand there with wide, unseeing eyes, seemingly unaware of the dreadful sounds issuing from her open mouth. Junko took one look at the ornate chaise-longue and then seized Hanae by the shoulders and shook her violently, controlling her own voice only with difficulty.

"Mrs Otani! Be quiet! Stop that noise this minute!" she said fiercely, then forcibly turned the older woman round and pushed her into an easy chair facing the wall. Her action broke the spell and Hanae sat slumped in the chair, her wails transmuted into low, sobbing moans. Junko grabbed a handful of paper handkerchiefs from an open box on the dressing table and thrust them roughly into her face. "Clean yourself up!" she ordered, and then bent over the grotesque reclining figure of Wesley Wilberforce.

He was propped against the end of the chaise-longue in such a way that the wig and great unwieldy head-dress of a Japanese bride remained perched on his head only slightly lop-sidedly, whilst the sumptuous folds of the richly decorated, heavy silk outermost kimono which he wore over his dark business suit had been arranged with some artistry, giving an impression of the seductive déshabille of a great courtesan of former times as depicted in wood-block prints. The purple, congested face too had been turned into a horrible, clownish parody of classical Japanese beauty, with daubs of thick white make-up plastered here and there and a slash of blood-red lipstick placed diagonally across the swollen lips.

The protruding eyes spoke clearly of death, but Junko nevertheless with difficulty untied and loosened the silken braid embedded in the flesh of Wilberforce's neck, and quickly tried and failed to find a pulse. The next part was hardest of all, and Junko had to clench her fists and close her eyes as she lowered her mouth to the painted, fleshy lips and tried the kiss of life. Somehow the revulsion passed and she fell into a rhythm, thinking furiously until she abruptly broke off and turned back to Hanae, now almost silent.

"Mrs Otani. This is Junko Migishima. You hear me? *Migishima*. Hyogo police. You must help me. Inspector Hara is in the audience. Go and bring him here. Inspector Hara! Fetch him! *Now*! Go!" Her voice cracked as she almost screamed the last words, but as she turned back to her grisly task she had the satisfaction of hearing Hanae get up and stumble out.

Then Junko was alone with the nightmare of what seemed a very long time before she heard the blessed sound of Hara's measured, pedantic tones, apparently comforting and re-assuring Hanae as they approached the room.

Chapter XIII

"All *right*. So she didn't turn up," Terry Phipps was saying to Hiroshi Uehara as he rounded the corner into the side corridor. "All I can say is we had lunch with that bitch Selena –" He stopped abruptly as he saw Kimura lounging elegantly against the closed door of Bridal Changing Room Number 7. "Oh *Christ*, not you again. Why don't you piss off? Nobody's going to give you an interview after that shambles."

He went to the room with Wesley Wilberforce's name on the door, wrenched it open and peered inside. "*Still* not back." The petulant little face swung back towards Uehara, ignoring Kimura. "Well, that's it. I've had enough. You can tell Her Ladyship from me when she deigns to put in an appearance. I'm finished. Going home. From now on she can find somebody else to hold her hot and sticky hand." Phipps disappeared inside and slammed the door behind him leaving Kimura alone in the corridor with Uehara, who was staring at him warily.

"Mr Phipps is under the impression that I'm a journalist, I

think," Kimura said, doing his best to sound casual. "Do I gather that the show wasn't a success?"

Uehara shook his head. "Quite the reverse. We all thought it went marvellously, and absolutely nothing untoward, thank goodness. . .except that Wesley Wilberforce didn't show up to take his bow with the others, which was a bit annoying."

"I can imagine. Know where he is?"

"I haven't the slightest idea. Excuse me, Inspector, but is there any way I can help you?"

"Well, you're politer than Mr Phipps, at least," Kimura said. "Yes, you can, as a matter of fact. Perhaps you'd be kind enough to ask all the people with rooms in this corridor to remain where they are for the next half hour with the doors closed. You'll find Mr Kubota in Mr Villon's room with him, I think. Madame Yasuda and Miss Norton are in their own rooms, and of course Terry Phipps is in Mr Wilberforce's. Perhaps you yourself would use Mr Kubota's temporarily. Borrow the key from him if it's locked. I'll let you know when you can all leave."

Uehara took a half step back and stared at Kimura, anxiety all at once back in his face. "Something *has* happened, Inspector. What is it? I insist on knowing."

"Nothing that need concern you at the moment. Please just do as I say. You can tell the others whatever you like. Tell them there's a surprise party being planned for all I care, but I want everybody to stay where they are. We have a little confidential business to attend to, and the sooner you let us get on with it the sooner we shall be finished." It was extremely difficult to maintain an outward appearance of nonchalance, and Kimura closed his eyes momentarily in relief when Uehara at last began to do as he was told and the door to Kubota's room eventually closed behind him.

Then he slipped hurriedly into the room where Hara was waiting for him and sent Migishima outside to stand guard in the corridor. Kimura was not looking forward to the next bit in the least and hoped very much that the suddenly masterful Hara knew what he was doing

99

"If you would be so kind as to take the lead, Inspector," Hara murmured to Kimura as the most prominent participants in Mode International entered the chaos of the main dressing-room ahead of them. "Everybody we need to talk to speaks or understands English, I believe, and it would be better. . ."

"By all means," Kimura said at once. It was a relief to be back in the land of the living, and his composure began to return as he set to work to do the sort of thing he knew he did best. He rapped loudly on the nearest table-top and raised his voice. "Ladies and gentlemen! May I have your attention, please? Would you be kind enough to come over to this corner of the room? It's not quite so cluttered and there are a few chairs about if you would care to sit down."

He managed a half-smile for Mie Nakazato as the women in a group centred on Kuniko Doi stared at him in some bewilderment and then began to do as they were bid, followed by those who had been temporarily imprisoned in their rooms and over whom an uneasy hush had fallen. Meantime Hara moved towards Junko Migishima and the Japanese staff still working and murmured something to them, at which they obediently retreated to the other end of the room and whispered among themselves as Hara rejoined Kimura.

"First of all I must explain to those of you who don't know us that my colleague and I are police officers. My name is Jiro Kimura and this is Inspector Takeshi Hara. Our special apologies to those of you we had to confine to your rooms for a while there. It was on account of a very sad occurrence. I regret to inform you, ladies and gentlemen, that Mr Wesley Wilberforce –"

He was interrupted by a strangled, sobbing wail from Terry Phipps, whose face was red and contorted, and who abruptly began to lunge forward until restrained by Kubota, who gripped the little man firmly by the upper arm with one hand and put his other arm seemingly protectively round his shoulders.

Kimura looked round at the expressions on the faces turned towards him and then went on. "Mr Wilberforce died suddenly this afternoon."

Chapter XIV

"Hey! Ezaki! Ezaki! Over here a minute. Yes, you. Over here." With the darkness a chill drizzle had set in, and a trickle found its way down the back of Tsutomu Kubota's collar as he froze into immobility for a long moment at the sound of his real name. Then he turned slowly in the direction of the hoarse whisper coming from the shadows at the side of the ornate porch of the Tamahimeden.

"Come on, then, haven't got all night. No, you won't need a taxi yet awhile."

The taxi drivers of Kobe knew all about Mode International, and for the past week there had been two or three waiting outside the entrance of the wedding hall for fares at most times during the day. It was a short, lucrative run to the shops, restaurants and three railway stations at Sannomiya, and there had been plenty of coming and going during the setting-up period. The pickings would be even better with the general public turning up in their hundreds for the advertised shows.

Kubota hesitated, then made a quick, negative gesture at the hopeful driver at the head of the line and moved towards the bulky man in the dark corner.

"That's better. Remember me? Shouldn't think so after all these years. Mind you, you've filled out a bit yourself too."

The designer had emerged from the Tamahimeden with his camel-hair topcoat loose over his shoulders like a cloak and put it on properly only when he saw the rain. Now he hunched into it as though for a different kind of protection as Noguchi whispered on remorselessly. "Been to see the doctor's wife since you've been back? Very proud of you, shouldn't wonder. Justified her faith, you might say."

This time Kubota's eyes opened wide in recognition and his mouth twisted into an attempt at a smile. "You. Inspector . . . what was it, Nogami?"

"Noguchi. They call me Ninja."

"Yes. I remember you now. I should have recognised you sooner. Nobody's called me Ezaki for years. Well, I must admit I never expected to see you again. You're still. . .?"

"With the police? Yes. You're in the big league now, though. Aren't you, Ezaki?"

Noguchi thrust his face close to Kubota's and grinned evilly as the younger man drew back at the smell of alcohol on his breath. "The old bastard's pissed, he's thinking to himself. He's wrong, though," he growled.

Kubota's expression remained one of distaste mingled with wariness and he looked at his watch ostentatiously. "Look," he said, "I don't know what all this is about, or why you're hanging about out here. I never expected to see you again in my life and I've got an appointment." He raised his arm to beckon to the taxi-driver who was continuing to keep an eye on them, and winced when Noguchi gripped and lowered it again.

"Wait. We'll just go for a little walk first. I want to know what you talked about."

Kubota tried unsuccessfully to shake himself free as Noguchi propelled him down the steps and towards the road.

"Talked about? What are *you* talking about? I'd never set eyes on the man until we arrived here and I've hardly exchanged two words with him since. I'm shocked, of course, but –"

"Come off it. I tailed you when you went to see him in the hospital earlier today."

Noguchi bundled Kubota along, hardly listening to his confused protestations. He wanted to get him well clear of the building before questioning him seriously; well out of earshot of the listening figure he had just spotted moving like a wraith in the shadows from which he himself had so recently emerged.

Kimura looked carefully into Terry Phipps' puffy face. His eyes were greenish grey and their bloodshot whites made them look eerily inhuman, for all the pathetic vulnerability of the Englishman's posture. As the evening wore on the rain had become heavier, and silvery streaks appeared from time to time on the single window of the poky little office of the head of the city hospital's administrative section. There was a third man with them in the room: the British vice-consul who, in response to Kimura's urgent message, had met them at the mortuary to witness the formal identification of Wesley Wilberforce's body. As Kimura continued to stare in silence the official stirred uneasily in his uncomfortable upright chair, making it creak. "Look here, Inspector," he said plaintively. "This hasn't been very nice even for me, let alone for Mr Phipps here. Couldn't this interview wait till morning?"

He was a stranger to Kimura. A thin, young-old man called Cooper, he had only recently arrived at the Consulate General in Osaka. Within a minute or two of meeting him at the hospital Kimura filed him in his mind as one of those who had come up through the ranks, too old in such a post to be one of the bright graduate "hard language" specialist diplomats serving out an apprenticeship in Osaka before moving to the more rarefied air of the Chancery in Tokyo. Cooper wore an elderly, nondescript suit shiny at the elbows

103

and seat, and a nervous expression. Kimura was not impressed, and spoke to him sharply.

"You and I are doing our jobs, Mr Cooper, and our personal feelings are irrelevant. And yes, I appreciate that this is very distressing for Mr Phipps. It was a great deal more so for the late Mr Wesley Wilberforce. I am involved in a murder investigation which has already begun, sir, and I have a number of questions to put to Mr Phipps. Not tomorrow, but now. I'm trying as it is to keep things brief by conducting this interview here rather than back at prefectural police headquarters. It's up to him whether he wishes you to be present or not. Well, Mr Phipps?"

When Terry Phipps did speak it was in little more than a whisper. "Get it over with, for God's sake."

"Right. And would you like Mr Cooper here to stay?"

"Suit yourself. Why should I care about anything, now that I've lost Wes?"

Cooper twitched unhappily, looked at his watch and half rose from his chair, only to subside again when Phipps rubbed at his inflamed eyes with one hand and put the other out to detain him. "Stay here. Please," he faltered, and then hunched over, buried his face in both hands and uttered an ugly keening sound ending in a choking sob.

It was stagey, Kimura thought, reminiscent of the larger-than-life emotionalism beloved by audiences at kabuki performances, but not at all like the camp, limp-wristed affectation he had observed with wry amusement when he had first encountered Phipps at the party after the Mode International press conference. "Drink some coffee, Mr Phipps," he advised briskly, reaching for his own paper cup. He had treated them all as they passed a dispensing machine in the waiting area outside the general office of the hospital: it was a predictably repulsive brew, but better than nothing.

Phipps sniffed several times and roused himself enough to sip some coffee, looking dully at Kimura as he did so. Kimura rubbed his hands together briskly. "All right. I'll try to keep it brief. And I'd appreciate straightforward answers. This matter is too serious for evasions. You were Mr Wilberforce's principal business associate and in public made no secret of the nature of your personal relationship with him. You were lovers, were you not?"

His eyes almost closed again, Phipps nodded. Kimura pressed on, ignoring the consul's expression of distaste and quickly suppressed gesture of protest. "That relationship was of many years' standing, wasn't it? Seventeen years, if I remember rightly?" Kimura sat back a little as Phipps nodded again and opened his mouth to speak.

"All those years," he said almost dreamily, and then straightened up and spoke more firmly and with a certain dignity. "I know what you're getting at. Try being a bit straightforward yourself. You think I killed Wes. Make a note of this. . . you too, Mr Cooper. I would have given my life for Wes, and anybody who knows us will tell you the same." His lips quivered and he hesitated before going on. "We were devoted. Since long before he got famous. . . he never did actually come out, couldn't really, not with the sort of clients he had, but all the same –"

"You lived together in London, I presume?"

Phipps shook his head slowly. "No. That was the only thing we ever quarrelled about. He had his flat above the work-rooms in Pont Street and made me stay tucked away over the river in Battersea. I could see the point before they changed the law, but. . ."

His tone suddenly changed, a hint of the exhibitionism which had seemed to Kimura to dominate his character before the murder flickering back as he clenched his fists and leant forward. "What the hell are you grinning about? My God, Wes is lying there in that fucking fridge, and you –"

"Calm down," Kimura said quietly. "Let's go back to your remark about quarrelling, shall we? Do you seriously want me to believe that you hardly ever quarrelled with Wilber-force? When I've heard you with my own ears walking about at a party complaining about him to anyone willing to listen, and threatening to leave him?"

"Look here, Inspector, I really must intervene. . ."
Cooper began timidly, only to recoil when Phipps rounded on
him.

"Oh, belt up, you! I can handle this jumped-up creep. You
fancy yourself, don't you?" he demanded, turning back to
Kimura. "A right smart-arse, poncing about pretending to be
a journalist, sticking your big ears into other people's private
conversations!"

"There was nothing private about your remarks, either
after the press conference or at the Japan-British Society
reception, Mr Phipps. Now control yourself and listen to me
for a while, or we really will continue this conversation at
headquarters. I accept that you're very upset over the death
of your friend, and I've no wish to distress you unnecessarily.
Nevertheless I have to make it clear to you, in the presence of
Mr Cooper here, that there are a number of witnesses to the
fact that on at least two recent occasions you have been heard
to say that your patience with Wilberforce was exhausted and
that you planned to walk out on him. Could it be that he made
you so angry today that something snapped and –"

The vice-consul was on his feet, spots of colour in his
otherwise pasty cheeks. "Inspector Kimura! This is all highly
irregular! If you have any reason to charge this British citizen
with a criminal offence I must insist on your doing so in the
proper manner. In any case I want you to know that I shall be
submitting a report about all this to my Consul-General,
and –" He spluttered into silence as Kimura stood up too.

"There is no formal charge against Mr Phipps," he said.
"He is – how do you put it in your country? – 'helping the
police with their enquiries'. And I was thinking aloud just
then. Let me offer one more thought which you might also
like to refer to in your report, Mr Cooper. When we had
gathered everybody together this afternoon at the Tamahimeden I made no mention of the fact that Mr Wilberforce
had been killed. I said only that he had died suddenly. Yet
before I'd even got that far Mr Phipps here reacted as though
he knew what I was going to say. Please sit down again, Mr

Cooper.I think we should both hear what Mr Phipps has to say."

Still obviously angry and offended, the consul nevertheless slowly resumed his seat and Kimura followed suit, breathing heavily.

Terry Phipps seemed to have crumpled, and to be occupying less space in the little room that he had before. When he spoke, though, he sounded more rational and controlled than he had at any other time since being brought to the hospital. "It wasn't a bit like you made it sound," he muttered. "I've always gone on like that about Wes. It was like – a sort of joke between us. Ask anybody. Ask Tracy. Ask Masako Yasuda, she's known us for years." He looked up, his face drawn with misery. "And as for this afternoon. . . when you said you were the police I had a premonition. I just *knew* something awful had happened to Wes. If you've ever been in love you'll know that's possible."

Kimura liked to think that he could always tell when a foreigner was dissembling, but Phipps bothered him, and the seeming sincerity of his new manner left him briefly at a loss. Furthermore, there was a technical problem to worry about. "Very well," he said lamely in the end. "We shall be wanting a formal statement from you tomorrow anyway, about your movements today and so on. In the meantime. . . Mr Cooper, may I have a word with you outside for a moment?"

Both Phipps and Cooper looked at Kimura with mingled hostility and distrust as he got up and went to the door, but eventually Cooper followed him out of the room and closed the door behind him. Kimura led him a few yards into the deserted and dimly-lit general office and spoke in an urgent undertone, keeping an eye on the vague outline of Phipps, visible through the reeded glass wall of the office they had just left.

"First, my apologies to you, Mr Cooper. I know you think I've been bullying Phipps. But murder is a serious matter, and one can't afford to be too tender about asking questions."

The official was still prickly, wearing the offended dignity of a weak and indecisive man out of his depth. "You weren't questioning him, Inspector. You were making serious accusations. Hang it all, I don't care for the man myself, but he's obviously overwrought –"

"That's the best time to talk to a suspect, Mr Cooper, and I must be quite frank with you, Phipps is a suspect. I'll take full responsibility for my actions when the time comes, but meantime I need your collaboration. Not only with the formalities over Wilberforce, but more urgently. I want to explain to you now in strict confidence that only Phipps among the Mode International people knows that Wilberforce was killed, or how. We've let the others assume that he died of a heart attack. Now if Phipps turns out not to have done it, then the actual killer also knows of course, and may unguardedly let the fact slip out. For that and other reasons my colleagues and I think it's worth keeping the details under wraps for as long as possible, anyway. I know I can count on your own discretion."

The vice-consul looked confused, but nodded his head slowly, and Kimura went on. "Right. That's why I'm going to have to pull Phipps in for a day or two. To ensure that he has no contact with any of the others. On the other hand I obviously don't want them to know he's in custody. So I want to give it out that he's in a state of shock and distress – which is true – and that you've invited him to stay with you for a day or two."

Cooper seemed to have mastered his sense of outrage, but now looked acutely unhappy. "Oh, but I don't think my wife would –"

"No, Mr Cooper, you've got me wrong. *We'll* take care of Phipps and make sure he's comfortable. And of course you'll have full consular access to him. All I want you to do is *pretend* he's staying with you and field any phone calls his friends may make – tell anyone who rings that Phipps is too upset to talk, something like that. Just for twenty-four hours or so. Will you do it? It may help us to catch the murderer of a British citizen."

Cooper seemed to squirm into himself as though mentally adopting a foetal position, and Kimura stared at him grimly, willing him to agree. "You could clear it with your Consul-General, of course," he suggested in the end, and was relieved when Cooper's expression brightened.

"Well, I suppose. . . provided my superiors agree. . ."

"Fine. I knew you'd see it my way. Right. Shall we go back in?"

When Kimura told Terry Phipps that the circumstances of Wilberforce's death were such that he had no alternative but to take him into custody for formal questioning, the reaction surprised him. Phipps made no protest. He even seemed to Kimura to look relieved.

Chapter XV

"Without doubt, Woman Senior Detective Migishima acted with commendable presence of mind, sir," Hara said firmly. "Had she raised the alarm herself or even come into the, ah, auditorium in search of me – leaving Mrs Otani once more alone in the presence of the body, I might add – it would have been virtually impossible for her to have preserved her cover. As it is, she can continue to observe the behaviour of several if not all the principals during the remainder of the week."

Otani looked at him sharply. "You don't mean to say they're going ahead with their wretched shows after this, do you?"

It was early the following morning, and although he had left Hanae looking and feeling much more herself than she had been in the confused aftermath of her traumatic discovery of Wilberforce's body, and although she had promised faithfully to stay quietly at home all day so that he could telephone her from time to time to find out how she was, Otani was nevertheless tetchy and on edge as he sat drinking cup after cup of green tea in his office with Hara, Kimura and Noguchi in attendance.

"Course they are," Noguchi put in unexpectedly. "Since Hara didn't tell the press anything about the fancy dress or mention murder. Quite right. 'Sudden Death'. Could be anything. Heart attack, whatever. That lot'll be glad of the publicity."

Otani switched his glare to his old friend. "You seem very sure about it, Ninja," he said coldly.

"I am. Had a word with young Ezaki – Kubota he calls himself now – last night. Told you I knew him years ago."

It was Kimura's turn to react. "For heaven's sake, Ninja, you might have told us you were in touch with him."

Noguchi poked a finger into his ear and worried at it as he turned his craggy head fractionally in Kimura's direction. "Telling you now," he growled.

Equally startled by Noguchi's announcement, Otani pulled himself together and sat up straighter in his chair. "All right, gentlemen. I'm looking forward to hearing what Ninja has to tell us myself, but let's go about this systematically and rationally, shall we? Just run over the main outlines of your report from the beginning again, Hara, and I don't want anyone to butt in except to clarify matters of fact. We can analyse the situation and make our own contributions when he's finished. Go ahead please, Inspector."

Hara inclined his head gravely and referred to the papers attached to his clip-board. Otani looked at the dark smudges under his eyes and, realising that he couldn't have had much sleep, reminded himself firmly not to interrupt and go off at a tangent. In spite of his stern warning he knew full well that he was consistently the worst offender in that respect.

"Thank you, sir. I will go over the background very briefly. We were all agreed that the incident at the drinks party immediately following the press conference in which Yutaka Watanabe was seriously injured and the subsequent discovery of evidence that the chandelier had been tampered with warranted a discreet police presence at the gala preview yesterday. In addition, that is, to Officer Migishima whose movements would necessarily be very restricted and who would be in no position to observe the public aspects of the proceedings. I discussed the matter further with Inspector Kimura, pointing out that in view of what we now know about the so-called extortion letter it would be desirable for Uehara and others responsible for the organisation of the show to be kept in ignorance of any arrangements we decided to make. The Inspector agreed that since he was now personally acquainted with several of those principally involved and would be recognised at once it would be better for him not to go to the preview. He therefore kindly allowed me to use his invitation card. In the event the reception arrangements were very perfunctory and I was able to slip past the desk at which complimentary souvenir programmes were being handed to guests who showed their cards. Apart from a few places set aside for specially distinguished guests, the seats were unreserved and I selected one conveniently near a door. I noticed Mrs Otani sitting not far away in front of me. The show commenced at three thirty-four p.m."

Having heard this part before, Otani drifted off into a brief reverie, wondering again why he had felt such a sense of foreboding when Hanae had told him of her intention to go to the preview, and remembering how difficult it had been to explain to her in her distress afterwards that he had feared that *something* disagreeable might happen there, but not by any stretch of the imagination that it would involve her so directly and so horribly.

Hara was quite right. Junko Migishima had behaved with exemplary professionalism and sensitivity. As soon as it became clear that Wilberforce could not be revived and Hara had summoned first the police medical adviser and then confidential reinforcements in the persons of Kimura and his assistant, Junko's husband, Junko escorted Hanae to the lobby. There she rang Otani on his own direct line and concisely reported what had happened. Otani had been at the Tamahimeden himself in less than ten minutes, by which time Junko had already been absent from her ostensible work in the dressing-room for nearly half an hour.

"So far as I could judge as a member of the audience, everything proceeded normally until four forty-three, when the show was nearing its end with the showing of the dresses of Madame Yasuda. Mrs Otani in a state of obvious distress appeared at my shoulder and asked me to go with her at once. I did so. The activity on the stage at the time was spectacular, and I doubt if our departure was remarked. Mrs Otani directed me to Bridal Changing-Room Number 7 where I found Woman Senior Detective Migishima administering artificial respiration in an attempt to revive the middle-aged foreigner subsequently identified as Wesley Wilberforce, who was in a reclining position on a sofa with only one end, which I subsequently learned is known as a chaise-longue. It must have been a repugnant task to her, especially as she was presumably aware from the outset that it was in the highest degree probable that Mr Wilberforce had been dead for some time. I commended Officer Migishima, but requested her to desist, it being clear to me even as a layman that nothing could be done for the victim. The circumstances being clearly indicative of foul play –".

"Now I must ask you to elaborate on that, Inspector. Remember that I didn't go to the room myself. Neither I nor of course Inspector Noguchi here saw the body. My wife described the scene to me as best she could, but. . ."

Hara nodded courteously. "I was about to come to that, sir. In making these notes I regret that I recorded a conclusion before citing the evidence which led me to it. Still loosely in place round the neck of the dead man was a length of *kumihimo* or woven silk braid known as an *obishime*. Obishime are of course used to secure the wide sash worn by women with the traditional kimono. They are, for your added information, between 130 and 150 centimetres long and can be either flat, usually about two centimetres wide, or cylindrical in section like a cord, and smaller."

He looked up and smiled bashfully. "My wife told me. She

113

makes them as a hobby," he added, then cleared his throat in an official way.

"The one round Mr Wilberforce's neck was of the cord type, less than a centimetre thick. Officer Migishima had of course loosened it before I arrived on the scene, but she states that, having heard disturbing sounds through the open door of the room while on her way back from the ladies' room to the main dressing-room adjoining the auditorium, she made her way to the source of the sound and found Mrs Otani in the presence of the body. At that time, she asserts, the obishime was tied so tightly as to have become partially embedded in the flesh and was secured with a knot, above which a decorative bow had been tied. When I first saw the body it was fully dressed in Western clothes, over which the outer kimono of a bridal costume had been placed. A bridal wig and head-dress had been placed on the head, and cosmetics crudely applied to the face and mouth. The right hand of the victim was crossed over the chest, clutching a small ceremonial dagger of the kind traditionally worn with bridal costume. I believe, sir, that it would have been physically impossible for Mr Wilberforce to have strangled himself and secured the obishime in the way described by Officer Migishima; still less to have disposed himself, dagger in hand, on the chaise longue in such a way as not to displace the wig and head-dress."

Otani managed a suitably chastened smile. "All right, you've made your point. Sorry I interrupted."

"Not at all, sir. I was myself at fault –" The look in Otani's eye halted Hara in mid-sentence and he began again. "Concluding that Mr Wilberforce was definitely dead, and on the reasonable assumption that he had been murdered, I judged it prudent for information about the circumstances of his death to be restricted to as few people as possible. I therefore telephoned to request the immediate assistance of the official medical examiner, of Inspector Kimura and his assistant Officer Migishima only. I then urged Mrs Otani to speak to nobody except Woman Senior Detective Migishima and yourself about the matter, sir, and she left the room –"

"With Junko-san. Yes. We all know and like the young lady, Hara. Since she and her husband are now both involved it will be simpler if you refer to her by her first name."

Hara looked scandalised but nodded and continued. "Woman Senior – I beg your pardon, sir. After a necessarily hurried consultation, Junko-san readily saw the force of my argument and agreed to return to the main dressing-room as soon as Mrs Otani was sufficiently recovered from her state of shock to be left to rest quietly, perhaps in the coffee shop in the basement. I did not authorise her to telephone you personally, sir, but in retrospect support her initiative in having done so –"

"So do I," Otani said curtly, and then repented. "I'm very glad she did," he added in a milder tone. "I do realise that you had plenty on your hands at the time and some quick thinking to do."

Hara took off his glasses and rubbed a hand over his eyes, which, bereft of their normal protection, looked tired and troubled. "While waiting for Inspector Kimura and the others to arrive I made a quick superficial examination of the room and then went outside, closed the door and remained in the side corridor. The fashion show must have ended by then since many people were passing the end of it on their way out. I saw nobody enter the side corridor, however, until Inspector Kimura and his assistant arrived."

"Thank you, Inspector. That's all pretty clear." Otani nodded in his direction and then turned enquiringly to Kimura. "Perhaps you might take up the story at this point, Kimura-kun. After you nearly knocked me down at the entrance, I mean."

"I'm sorry about that, Chief –"

"It's all right, you apologised at the time and gave a perfectly reasonable explanation of the hurry you were in. I would have joined you if I hadn't had to look after my wife."

Having arrived at the Tamahimeden and once satisfied that Hanae was in a rational state of mind and unhurt physically,

Otani had in fact been sorely tempted to leave her in the care of Junko Migishima while he went on to the scene of the crime himself and was still regretting the fact that he had not done so. Junko must have read his mind, though, because she extricated herself neatly but firmly from their presence and disappeared from the lobby just as Kimura hurtled in through the door with Migishima in his wake and barged at first unseeingly past Otani as he rushed to the reception desk to enquire the whereabouts of Bridal Changing-Room Number 7.

"Yes. I thought you might have had that in mind when I recognised you and came back from the reception desk to apologise. I'm glad I persuaded you that it would be better to take Mrs Otani home and listen to her account of what happened. It was better not to have too many people in and around the room, especially when the doctor turned up and we had to get hold of the manager and brief him confidentially what had happened."

"Get on with it." Noguchi's growl was as peremptory as usual when directed at Kimura, who shot a wounded glance in his direction and then carried on, more in the formal style Hara had used. "When I joined Hara the scene was as he has described it. He explained what he proposed and I agreed completely with his suggestions. When the doctor arrived he and Hara stayed in the room and I hung about in the corridor noting the names on some of the doors and waiting for their occupants to put in an appearance. Wondering what was keeping them, in fact, though Junko-san told us later that they'd all been drinking champagne in the main dressing-room with the models. She'd been able to slip back in without anybody commenting on her absence, it seems. Eventually Marian Norton, the American designer, came into the corridor and went straight into her own room. I'd not met her personally and I don't think she noticed me particularly. The same applied to the Frenchman Jean-Claud Villon who arrived a minute later with Madame Yasuda and Kubota, all talking French. That is to say, I'd not spoken to any of them

116

before, but Madame Yasuda must have known who I was, having arranged for Uehara to talk to me after the original briefing meeting at the City Hall.''

"I see. Did any of them seem nervous or agitated, anything like that?"

"Not that I noticed, Chief. Masako Yasuda gave me a black look as if to say 'What the hell are you doing here?' but that was all. Villon opened the door of his own room and they all stood there for a minute, then Yasuda peeled off and went into her own room and Kubota went into Villon's with him. It was Terry Phipps who seemed to be in an agitated state – he showed up next, with Uehara. And of course he was the one personally closest to Wilberforce. So it made sense to take him along to the mortuary to do the formal identification, and er. . . then it became necessary to quarantine him as it were –''

"We'll come back to that extraordinary. . . initiative of yours later," Otani cut in grimly. "Go back to Uehara's reaction when you made everybody stay in their rooms."

"Well, of course he didn't like it a bit. First he blustered and demanded an explanation. Then he simmered down and began to look more and more uneasy, and in the end he did what I said," Kimura went on apprehensively. "There was no alternative, Chief. The corridor more or less had to be sealed off for a while if we were to keep the details dark. Fortunately the photographer arrived soon after that. He got to work as soon as the doctor had finished and took a complete set of pictures of the whole set-up before the wedding gear was taken off the body. I put Migishima on guard in the corridor while Hara and I got most of the make-up off the face – horrible job that was – and covered the head and neck before the ambulance men brought a stretcher and took the body away to the municipal hospital. There's no way of keeping the fact that Wilberforce certainly didn't die a natural death from the staff at the morgue, but I think we can be reasonably certain that the original creepy scene in that room is at present known only to Mrs Otani, Junko-san, her

117

husband, the doctor, our own photographer, us in this room, Phipps – and of course the murderer if it *isn't* him. The kimono, head-dress, wig and so on – and the obishime and dagger of course – are at the regional forensic lab. Hara and I decided against sealing the room. It would have needed too much explaining. It's locked, of course, but that doesn't mean a thing with all the pass-keys there must be knocking about the place." Kimura paused and looked at Hara for confirmation.

Hara nodded and took up the story again. "Thanks to the manager's efficient cooperation, the removal of the body was achieved quite unobtrusively, sir. Fortunately the journalists who had been present at the show were for the most part fashion writers rather than reporters. They had all left the premises immediately after it finished, with the exception of Miss Mie Nakazato of the *Kobe Shimbun* and Miss Selena Stoke-Lacy, a fashion writer from England. These two ladies were in the main dressing-room talking to Miss Kuniko Doi and the models Miss Vanessa Radley and Miss Barbi Mingus when Inspector Kimura and I assembled the others there. I refer of course to Madame Yasuda, Miss Norton, and Messrs Villon, Kubota and Phipps. All the other models had left by then, but some of the staff were still clearing up. Including, ah, Junko-san, of course."

"After I announced that Wilberforce was dead they all started talking at once, didn't they, Hara?" Hara sat back as Kimura cut in, took off his glasses and rubbed his eyes again.

"Hardly surprising, I should have thought," Otani commented drily. "Nothing that you could take it into your head to do could surprise me now, Kimura, but I can't understand why you lent yourself to this elaborate performance, Hara, still less suggested it in the first place. It's like something out of a *misuteri* novel."

Otani was addicted to crime fiction and, uncharacteristically for a conservatively-minded Japanese who viewed most foreigners with a fairly jaundiced eye, he preferred translations from Western writers to the domestic product. He was

118

a particular admirer of Simenon, and in lighter moments much enjoyed Emma Lathen and the late Rex Stout, envying Nero Wolfe his sybaritic life-style but finding that pushing his lips out and in did nothing to help his own thought-processes. In spite of his continuing anxiety over Hanae and chagrin at not having been in on the act at the Tamahimeden himself, he was cheering up and inventing *misuteri* titles for the present case in his head. *Death by Design* would be rather neat, he thought, still gazing expressionlessly at Hara. "Did you expect the murderer to go pale and pull out a gun? Or jump out of the window?"

It was the first time Hara had been subjected to this kind of sarcastic chivvying from Otani, and he hesitated painfully after opening his mouth to reply.

Inured to it, Kimura smiled tightly and responded for him. "Not quite, Chief, no. Phipps was in a highly emotional state, more or less out of control. Uehara looked pretty shattered, but then Junko-san reported after her first day there that he was going about looking very haggard. It could have been sheer exhaustion, plus anger because I hadn't told him in advance. As for Masako Yasuda – well, I certainly wouldn't put it past her to have dreamed up the extortion swindle in the first place. She has a poker face as good as your own, if I may say so. I didn't notice any other reactions in particular. There were quite a lot of people there, after all, and one could only get a quick impression. Did you pick up anything significant, Hara?"

Thus appealed to, Hara blinked furiously. "Kubota was very quick to restrain Phipps when it seemed he might break down – which was, incidentally, before you actually said Wilberforce was dead. And the Frenchman actually *smiled*, if I'm not mistaken."

Otani sat up straight. "Yes. If I've got my arithmetic right, you had something like ten or eleven people assembled there. I'm bound to say I'm amazed either of you thought you'd achieve anything very dramatic with your bombshell with so many to keep an eye on."

119

"That wasn't really the objective, Chief." Kimura sounded hurt. "There was no harm in watching their immediate reactions, certainly, but the main point of our tactics was to keep quiet about the manner of death and Wilberforce's weird appearance. We shall be interviewing everyone individually, and hoping that somebody will slip up and inadvertently admit knowing something he or she shouldn't."

"There's no harm in hoping, I suppose, but all the same, I – oh, never mind." Otani said, pushing back his cuff to look at his watch. "Time's getting on. What happened next? Let's keep it brief, shall we?"

"I'll try. Uehara was the first to ask how Wilberforce died, though both Kuniko Doi and Vanessa Radley came back to the point later. My reply to all of them was simply that it seemed to have been some kind of seizure, but that there would have to be a post mortem. It was Madame Yasuda who told Uehara to rush out a press release and under the circumstances we could hardly forbid it. In any case Miss Nakazato was already there representing the *Kobe Shimbun*. Hara reminded me to ask people how Wilberforce had seemed when they last saw him – this was to establish when he was in fact last seen publicly, of course. I'd heard Phipps mention earlier in conversation with Uehara that he'd lunched with Miss Stoke-Lacy and Wilberforce. A bit confusing, actually, because he habitually refers to Wilberforce as though he was a woman. Neither of them said anything – Phipps was still practically hysterical, with Kubota trying to calm him down. However, there seemed to be a vague consensus that Wilberforce *had* put in an appearance in the dressing-room before the show began. Vanessa Radley said that he seemed fine when he wished her luck. No doubt the other models will be able to confirm that he was there."

"No need. Ask Junko-san."

"I have already done so, sir, and she confirms it. Later today I shall take her through the whole sequence of events as she saw them. Her observations will no doubt be of the greatest assistance as the investigation proceeds."

120

Kimura nodded in agreement with Hara and then shrugged. "Well, that more or less wrapped it up, although there was a lot more confusion before we let them all except Phipps disperse."

Otani rubbed his nose. "You really thought that one of those – what is it, nine, ten – people did it? Shouldn't you have interviewed them separately right away?"

"We agreed that some of those the Inspector spoke to can be ruled out, sir," Hara said. "After Mr Wilberforce was last seen in the dressing-room the models, for example, were at all times either there or on stage. Miss Doi was on stage throughout the show –"

"But he could have been killed before the show began," Otani pointed out. "And what about this English fashion writer woman? Or even your young lady friend from the *Kobe Shimbun*, Kimura. They could come and go pretty freely behind the scenes, I imagine?"

Kimura straightened himself in his chair and exchanged a weary look with Hara. "We're not assuming *anything*, Chief," he said carefully. "We can't draw a line round any group of people and say that one of them must have done it; I only wish we could. We had to make a start somewhere, though. Wilberforce was killed in a very, well, *showy* sort of way, which at least suggests a complicated personal motive. Even though we're dealing with foreigners, all experience suggests that we should begin at home, as it were. That's why I began with his assistant, friend, lover, whatever. Phipps."

"Yes. Stop right there, Kimura. I want a better answer to certain questions than you gave me in that incoherent telephone call yesterday evening. I'm quite expecting the British Consul-General to complain at any moment to the Foreign Ministry liaison office in Osaka about your actions. It will be as well if I know what to say when he does."

Kimura visibly braced himself to launch into an extended defence of his actions, but Otani raised a hand before he could begin. "I know *what* you did. And it's too late now to undo it. My main question is this. Why, if you automatically

121

assumed that Phipps is the most likely one to have killed the other Englishman because of their relationship, did you tell him and him alone that he had been murdered? If you're right, it ought to have been easy to trap him into the sort of verbal slip you've been going on about. As it is, he hasn't confessed and now he's fully on guard."

Kimura's face was a study in chagrin. "I know. I'd planned to say nothing to him either, and just keep a very careful eye on his reaction when confronted with the body for identification. The moment Phipps was shown the dead man's face in the mortuary, though, he grabbed the sheet and pulled it down. The marks round the neck were so obvious it was impossible to keep up a pretence after that."

"I see," Otani said. "And his reaction persuaded you that he isn't in fact the guilty man?"

"Well, yes. I'm convinced Phipps knows something, but if he actually did kill Wilberforce he's an actor of genius. I'd not intended to arrest him unless he confessed on the spot or otherwise made it obvious that he'd done it, but after what happened I had to think in terms of one of the others and still give the plan Hara and I had agreed on a chance of working. That's why I acted as I did."

"And what, may I ask, do you propose to do now? Question Phipps again, I presume?"

Otani's manner towards Kimura was still frosty and both Hara and Noguchi remained silent as Kimura shifted in his seat and nodded. "Yes, sir," he said formally. "I'm hoping to get some ideas about possible motivation from him. At the same time extend the enquiry outwards, to take in Wilberforce's closest professional associates here, namely the other designers. We'll have to talk to a lot of people, including practically everybody working behind the scenes. Some we shall be able to eliminate. Others will perhaps suggest other leads –"

"That is so, sir. Bearing in mind, of course, the possibility that the incident of the chandelier is relevant. . . that perhaps Wilberforce and not Watanabe was the intended victim."

122

Kimura was grateful for the intervention, and as Hara earnestly outlined his own proposed tactics for the next stage of the investigation, he allowed his mind to drift back to the mystery of Selena's behaviour.

Odd that Otani should have mentioned her even casually as a possible suspect. As matters stood Kimura was reluctant to confuse the issue further by reporting his abruptly interrupted conversation with her following the Japan-British Society reception. She had a lot of explaining to do anyway, and especially in the aftermath of Wilberforce's death. There were a great many other things he intended to ask her in the formal context of a police interview in addition to whether she still feared for Kubota's life, and if so, why.

"I'm sure you agree, Kimura-kun."

Kimura jerked himself back to the present as it sank in that he was being spoken to, and rapidly focused on Otani. The tone of voice had been friendly enough, and he inferred with relief that Otani had accepted his reasons for arresting Phipps. "Yes, of course," he hastened to agree as invited.

"Kubota must have been caught thoroughly off balance," Otani went on. "Though I do feel that we ought to try to coordinate these initiatives more systematically." The remark scarcely constituted a snub, but Noguchi raised an eyebrow and seemed about to take offence. Otani was in no mood to indulge him, though. "Well, what did he say then, Ninja?"

Noguchi began to haul himself into a more upright posture, but soon sagged back comfortably again. "It was a matter of cross-purposes, see? I was talking about Watanabe, he thought I was on about this fairy Wilberforce. But I didn't know anything about that at the time. I'd had a useful day digging round Watanabe. And Ezaki himself, while I was at it."

"Can we please agree to refer to him as Kubota?" It had turned into a long session and Otani was fretting again, wanting to reassure himself that Hanae was all right. "There are quite enough people in this case as it is without aliases thrown in."

"Kubota then. Not staying with his family. Too good for them these days. At the New Port Hotel, he is. A bit run down these days in my opinion, but handy for the wedding hall." Noguchi paused and fixed his tortoise eye on Hara before going on.

"Been keeping an eye on him for you. Walked over for breakfast in the coffee shop at the Oriental with Yasuda yesterday, he did. Then a long session in Yamaichi Securities by the station there. Lunch with Uehara in that pricey eel restaurant in the underground shopping centre, and then off to the Kaigan Hospital. Makes you think."

"Maybe. I'm hanged if I know *what*, though," Kimura said plaintively. "Did he tell you what he talked to Watanabe about? He's had a set-back, by the way, according to the nursing sister I spoke to on the phone first thing. Was progressing quite well considering his age, but now they've got him in intensive care."

"Well, Ninja? Did Kubota tell you that too?" Otani was becoming increasingly twitchy.

"No. Said they talked about the weather. Results of the last baseball season. Watanabe follows the Yomiuri Giants, it seems. Purely friendly visit. Bunch of grapes. So he said. How did he come to know Watanabe in the first place, I said. No answer. Wish I'd known this other guy had copped it, could have leant on him. Anyway, had to let him go in the end. Kubota took a bit of trouble trying to lose me. Amateurish. Spotted this classy bit of foreign crumpet trying to keep out of sight outside the Tamahimeden while I was working on Kubota. Well, he ended up at that Mexican restaurant up at Kitano and there she was waiting for him inside. Doubt if they had much of an appetite by then."

Chapter XVI

"I'm quite all right now. Really. You mustn't worry about me any more." Hanae smiled at her husband from the gateway as he turned round from fastening the sliding front door and patted his breast pocket to make sure that he had his wallet with him. "You'll spoil me, what with the reception in Osaka and now taking me out for supper."

All the same, she was thoroughly glad to escape from the house. Otani was not a demonstrative man, but his concern on the comparatively rare occasions during their married life when she had been ill or greatly upset had always been as overwhelming as it was touchingly incompetent. It would have been out of the question for her to have tried that morning to explain that the best way to banish the ghastly scene in the room at the Tamahimeden from her imagination, at least for a while, would be to go to Osaka or Kobe and look at the shops.

Instead she had been confined to the house, prowling about finding unnecessary jobs to do and fielding a total of four anxious telephone calls from him, each of which had the effect of making her re-live the moment when she stood by the chaise-longue, as though paralysed, heard her own voice beginning to rise unbidden, and realised that she had lost control. It had cost Hanae a lot to greet Otani on his eventual arrival home with a fair imitation of her customary pleasure, but there had been nothing simulated about her reaction to his invitation to her to put her coat on and walk down the hill to the local restaurant they sometimes used, generally for Saturday or Sunday lunch.

It had been a dull, rainy day except for the last half hour towards sunset, but the evening air smelt fresh and clean and Hanae sniffed it appreciatively as they set out at a good pace, thinking that she might after all be able to manage a small breaded pork cutlet as well as the miso soup and rice that came with it. "No phone calls, then," Otani said abruptly, as though he were making an announcement rather than asking a question.

"No. Except for yours, of course. I was rather hoping there'd be a letter from Akiko today, but then I expect she must be very busy getting ready to leave London." Otani made a neutral grunting sound, and although he seemed to be listening as Hanae went on to wonder aloud how well and quickly their grandson would settle down to primary school in Japan, he remained uncommunicative until they were settled in the restaurant at one of the tables rather than up at the counter and had ordered their meal.

There were only three other customers in the place, all men on their own, and all immersed in well-thumbed comic magazines from the pile kept on a table by the pink pay telephone near the door, even though the television set on a high shelf beside the counter was tuned to a currently popular samurai serial which held most of the attention of the proprietor-chef and his wife. A confrontation was taking place between a scowling feudal lord and the heroic retainer who questioned the justice of the taxes he was exacting from his starving peasants. The expressions on the faces of the

126

other officials in attendance suggested that the hero's summary execution was imminent, but the dénouement was postponed by a commercial break, and the familiar features of a much-loved retired sumo wrestler appeared on the screen. He was dressed in baby pyjamas and bouncing on the brand of futon he recommended.

Hanae had her back to the TV but the spectacle seemed to unlock Otani's tongue. "Well," he said. "I'm glad you're feeling better. Would it help to talk about it, or would you prefer to try to forget the whole thing?" The arrival at their side of the proprietor's wife with their food gave Hanae a few moments to prepare her reply.

"We *must* talk about it," she said eventually as Otani doused his golden-brown deep-fried breaded cutlet with brown sauce. "In the first place, I shall never be able to forget it as long as I live, but I think that talking about it may help me to come to terms with it. You've seen a lot of even more awful sights, I'm quite sure. So have most people in the police. That nice young Mrs Migishima, for instance. She didn't lose her head like me, and she's younger than Akiko. I've had a very protected life, and it's time I realised that frightful things don't only happen on television. What's more to the point though is that you are responsible for making sure that whoever killed that poor man so horribly is caught. Until that happens you'll be thinking about it a lot and it might help *you* to talk about it."

Otani nodded with a slight smile. "You're right. It might at that. Let's have another flask of sake, shall we?" He managed to catch the proprietor's eye and waved the empty one at him hopefully.

"You're being very philosophical about it all, I must say. I don't know whether you'd have been flattered or horrified this morning. We'd been over the whole thing you see, deciding where to start with the questioning and so forth. And as the meeting was breaking up I said to Hara that I assumed he hadn't got you on his list of suspects. Bit of a joke to lighten the atmosphere. Oh, dear. He blinked a lot and cleaned his glasses and then solemnly said no, that on the whole he didn't think you'd have had time to do it. He spotted you trying to hide behind your programme as soon as he arrived for the show, you see, and again when you slipped out with your tummy trouble. And believe it or not, he noted both the time you went out and the time you came back to fetch him. So congratulations, Madam. You're in the clear."

"That *is* a relief, I must say." Hanae did well to manage so light a response.

She was sure that her heart had missed a beat, and it was as though a cold hand was menacingly caressing her spine as her husband rambled on.

"Extraordinary fellow, but there's no doubt he's a professional to his fingertips. I still can't understand how it is that he and Ninja Noguchi get on so well together."

"Perhaps, perhaps since his son died Noguchi-san has felt lonely. He might think of Hara as, as. . . his adopted family." Hanae meant what she said but the faltering words came out without conscious thought on her part. She was still trying to assimilate the idea that Hara could conceive of her as a possible murderer, and to accept that he had struck her off the list of suspects on purely technical grounds.

"I'm glad I'm not involved in police work," she said after a comforting mouthful of sake. "It must be depressing to have to accept that even people you know personally might easily be criminals." Her lips were trembling slightly and Otani looked at her steadily.

"I'm sorry, Ha-chan," he said. "That was stupid of me. Of course he never for a second seriously thought you might have done it. In a case like this an investigating officer is only too glad to be able to eliminate people from the field. The more the better, but properly eliminated they must be, whoever they are and however nice they are. So cheer up, we're all on the same side. In fact, if you really don't mind talking about it, I'd like you to tell me again exactly what happened from the time you arrived at the Tamahimeden for the show and the moment Junko-san found you in that room. Even after that.

128

Until we left the building together to go home. You see, you might remember some detail, something you saw or heard perhaps without noticing it particularly at the time. It could help us a great deal."

Hanae gave her head a little shake and smiled ruefully. "I can try, I suppose. I'd rather be questioned by you than by Hara-san. I'd be afraid he was going to pull out a pair of handcuffs at any minute. Give me a little time to get into the right frame of mind, though. Why don't you tell me what sort of day you've had? Busy, I expect."

Otani saw no need to rush her, and in any case found it helpful to order his own thoughts as he embarked on a summary of his long sessions with Kimura, Noguchi and Hara. The instalment of the samurai epic on the television came to an end in a suitably cliff-hanging fashion. The banished hero, ambushed by his former colleagues, had drawn his sword to face appalling odds in the interests of the suffering peasants, having been persuaded to champion them on a full-time basis by the village headman's tragically beautiful daughter on whom the feudal lord had cast lecherous eyes.

The next programme was a quiz show chaired by a well-known professor of political science, and Otani interrupted himself long enough to draw Hanae's attention to his beaming countenance and comment that in his young days the idea of a smiling professor would have been unimaginable. Hanae had to agree. She had cared for her father-in-law from the time of her marriage until his death twelve years later, and neither before nor after the eminent scientist's retirement had she once seen anything other than a grave, dignified expression on his face. The same was true of his former colleagues, old gentlemen who came to call on him occasionally wearing kimono with long underwear visible at the ankles and surmounted by trilby hats, or panamas in summer.

"Well, as you can imagine there was plenty for everyone to do," Otani went on eventually, toying with his cup of green tea. Their meal was long finished, but it is only at lunchtime

129

that the staff of restaurants in Japan ever betray the slightest hint of a desire to see the backs of their patrons. "Kimura saw the dead man's assistant again and then went over to the Tamahimeden to interview the other foreigners, and Hara made a start on the Japanese." He sighed. "Ostensibly following up the chandelier business now that Watanabe is on the danger list, and hoping to trick somebody into admitting they know more about Wilberforce's death than they should. I'm not at all happy about this scheme of theirs but I agreed to let them try it, at least. Ninja thought it might be useful to check up on Kubota's dealings with the Yamaichi Securities people, and I agreed. He knows somebody there, it seems. I seem to have been landed with the Watanabe end of things. The manager of the Kobe branch of the Wakamatsu department store came to see me on behalf of the directors in Tokyo. A courtesy call, he said, but he'd obviously been briefed to try find out whether we thought it had been an accident or not. I got rid of him, and then had a chat with the Rotarian who arranged for Watanabe to give that talk at Rotary a few weeks ago. Oh, and I rang a few people in Tokyo. So you see we've all been chasing about, but we haven't had a chance to compare notes yet. I told Hara and Kimura both to get some rest this evening. . . they look exhausted. Junko Migishima rang in to report that the three shows went off without incident at the Tamahimeden. At eleven, two and five, and the same for the next few days. Then the whole circus is supposed to disperse, so we don't have them all together for very long. Good heavens, look at the time. We ought to be going, I suppose."

They took their time over the homeward walk up the steep hill to the old house, Mount Rokko looming dark and secretive above them. It was not yet quite nine in the evening but there were very few people about in the residential streets, and the owners of the little neighbourhood grocery shops were mostly beginning to put up the shutters. Otani offered no theory about the identity of the murderer and Hanae did not expect him to. The experience of many years

130

had taught her that in the course of the investigation her husband habitually leapt to conclusions he later rejected, and that he liked to brood over possibilities in his own way before sharing his considered thoughts with her.

In all their life together there had been only two or three occasions when he had questioned her closely about matters which bore on his professional concerns, and she would never forget them. The prospect of submitting herself to another such inquisition was disturbing and yet in a curious way exciting. The previous evening didn't count; then Otani had comforted her in her shock and distress and merely let her blurt out whatever occurred to her. This time she knew that her memory would be stripped and probed with delicate ruthlessness. It would be a kind of violation, but one she would yield to gladly, welcoming his invasion of her mind for the sake of the exhausted peace she believed would follow when he was done with her.

"Oh, before I forget," Otani said as they turned into their street. "I had a phone message from Mr Kosugi. You know, the chairman of the organising committee. They'll be sending a van tomorrow morning from the exhibition site to pick up our three best bonsai for the display. And others in the neighbourhood, of course. About ten. Mr Kosugi will be supervising everything personally, so they'll be well taken care of. I'll check and label them before I leave in the morning."

Chapter XVII

"Now this," Kimura said earnestly as he manipulated the keyboard of his newest toy. "is what we call a SWOT analysis." He was a keen reader of magazines aimed at high-flying urban business executives, and had lusted after the sleek little computer in its own slim-line attaché case from the moment he saw the advertisement. Its acquisition had justified a day trip to Tokyo a couple of weekends beforehand, because by buying it from one of the hundreds of discount stores piled high with electronic gadgetry and crowded cheek by jowl in the Akihabara district there he had saved more than twice the cost of his return fare on the bullet train.

A simple grid design glowed into green existence on the screen and he beamed proudly at Mie Nakazato, happy that he seemed to be getting the hang of the thing at last and that she had accepted his invitation to spend the evening with him. Mie was sitting in an unconsciously defensive posture beside him on the sofa in his "luxury flat" in Kobe at about the time the Otanis left home in quest of their pork cutlets, and

132

looking warily from time to time at the large *jinto* or gin-and-tonic Kimura had poured for her.

"Based on four English words. S for Strengths, W for Weaknesses, O for Opportunities and T for Threats. SWOT. It's a technique they use in planning marketing campaigns, and the moment I read about it I realised that with very minor adaptations it's a perfect analytical method for criminal investigation work. Take a murder for instance," he said, and paused as though about to choose a happier example before pressing on. "It's obviously essential to assess the relative weight of suspicion falling on each person associated with the victim. The S and W bits we can interpret in terms of motivation, or alternatively qualifications as a potential murderer. Opportunities speaks for itself, and we can think of Threats either in terms of the danger posed for the suspect by some activity of the victim – or knowledge possessed by the victim I suppose, though these would overlap with motivation, come to think of it – and plot the suspect's relative position on the grid. Get them all on the computer, you see. That's half the battle. The bottom left-hand corner of the grid is 'down' – meaning low ranking, while the top right-hand square is 'up', obviously." Kimura looked at Mie with kindly condescension. "Of course, you can also use this kind of grid arrangement for what people in business call a Boston Box, in which case the bottom right-hand corner would be called Dogs."

"Dogs?" Mie mouthed the word, a puzzled expression on her face.

"Yes. Dogs. Come on, you studied English for six years like everybody else. *Inu.*"

"Yes, I know what the word *means*. But why?"

"Why what?"

"Why is the bottom right-hand corner called Dogs?"

"Why? How should I know why? It just is, that's all. Now, watch this. We'll start with. . . oh, Mister X, say. Of course, as a matter of fact in most murder cases it's perfectly obvious who did it. They ring up or go to the police station and give

133

themselves up. That's when it's in the family. With gangsters we usually just get hold of one of the usual informers and pay for the name, but unfortunately. . ."

Mie tried to be attentive as Kimura muttered to himself, tapping keys, and the cursor veered and wandered over the screen like an errant comet in a children's cartoon film. Although now that she worked on a newspaper her sophistication was rapidly increasing to match her intelligence, she was quite prepared to believe that police methods involved the use of arcane techniques, and to acknowledge Kimura's authority and experience in his professional field.

The fact that she had understood scarcely a word of his explanation of his present manipulation of his pretty new computer, and even the drama of his announcement the previous day of the death of Wesley Wilberforce, did not dominate her thoughts. They were chiefly occupied by the recollection that on the last occasion she had been in Kimura's surprisingly comfortable and well-kept flat, and indeed beside him on that very sofa, she had found it extremely difficult to resist her own urgent desire to act on Kimura's suggestion that she should telephone her mother in Kyoto and explain that a very early assignment for the paper the next day made it essential for her to stay in Kobe overnight. In agreeing to meet him at his flat that evening to "have a few drinks and an omelette or something" Mie had accepted in her own mind that she had held Kimura off long enough and that, unless she was prepared to break off the relationship altogether, the moment of decision had come. She had even taken the precaution of warning her mother that she would probably be very late and had thought about what to say if and when she telephoned her again that evening. Now, taking a deep breath, she reached for her drink and swallowed a third of it with a devil-may-care sense of commitment.

Kimura did not seem to notice. He peered sharply at the glowing screen, tapped a few times at the same key and then referred for some time to the instruction leaflet which he took

134

from its special pocket in the lid of the case. Then with a decisive air he pressed another key and watched as with a discreetly modern sound a small square of paper began to emerge from the bowels of the machine. When the subdued clattering stopped he ripped the paper out, nodded thoughtfully as he first scanned it and then tucked it away in an inside pocket.

"So far, so good," he remarked mysteriously, switched the computer off and shut it away. "Now, here we are and with any luck we shan't be disturbed. So, what can you offer me?" Mie had been eyeing him quite tenderly over the rim of her glass but now the colour rose upwards from her throat to her cheeks and she recoiled from the uncharacteristic crudity of his approach. After another drink or two she would be ready to kiss him, but. . .

"I mean, did you get any indications from the models when you interviewed them about how they really thought about the designers? Wilberforce especially, needless to say." Kimura at last seemed to notice something odd about the expression on Mie's face. "I read your piece in this morning's paper, of course," he added hastily. "I thought it was really good."

"Thank you." Relieved and at the same time a little cross with Kimura, Mie concentrated on her drink.

Kimura waited for a second or two with an encouraging smile on his face, then as she made no further comment babbled on afresh. "I felt awful yesterday afternoon having to talk to you at the same time as all the others like that. Tell you about Wilberforce, I mean. I wanted to ask you to wait for me so that we could have a chat, but we were really very busy and what with one thing and another. . . and then today my colleague Hara and I have been tied up with meetings and interviews. It was a miracle you were there when I did manage to get to a phone. Did you go to the Tamahimeden today by any chance?"

"Yes. Kuniko Doi rang the office this morning and asked for me. I was quite excited when she said she'd read my piece about Vanessa Radley too and offered to give me an exclusive interview between the first and second shows. At about half-past twelve. Of course I jumped at the chance."

"Oh," Kimura said flatly. When deciding on tactics with Hara he had argued that Kuniko Doi should be on his list of interviewees along with Terry Phipps, Marian Norton, Jean-Claud Villon and Selena Stoke-Lacy, but Hara had stood firm and claimed all the Japanese for himself. At least, he insisted, until the second round after some had been eliminated and the situation would in any case need to be considered afresh. By the time Kimura had finished for the time being with Phipps, talked to both Cooper and the British Consul-General, contacted the immigration authorities and finally arrived at the Tamahimeden himself, it was already after two and the second Mode International show of the day had already begun.

"She really is a marvellous person," Mie said. "Obviously very upset about the murder, and couldn't imagine why you and Inspector Hara hadn't told everybody yesterday. Well, none of us could. Why didn't you, by the way?" Kimura shrugged, then sat up very straight and looked at her sternly. He was stimulated as always when involved in an investigation of the affairs of the Westerners whose patterns of thought and behaviour so intrigued him, but was conscious of weariness lying in wait somewhere, ready to bludgeon him into carelessness when he least expected it to. Now it was with a touch of embarrassment that he reminded himself that Mie Nakazato was a working journalist, albeit a very junior one. It had been foolish on his part to talk about murder while showing off with his computer.

"Look, I really would like your help, but all this is strictly off the record, right? They've explained to you at the *Kobe Shimbun* about that convention?"

"Yes. Off the record. Of course."

Reassured by her earnest nodding, Kimura hauled himself to his feet and took Mie's empty glass over to the side table on which he kept his collection of bottles and addressed her over

136

his shoulder as he made her another jinto, realising with part of his mind as he did so that he had said something about an omelette. He wondered whether Mie would mind if instead he were to ring the sushi shop and ask them to send round a couple of "special superior" boxes, or even a mixed selection for three or four persons in one of their fancy lacquer containers to make sure there would be more than enough for the pair of them. Sushi went extremely well with gin and tonic, he always thought, and knew that he always had room for more than the standard portion for one.

"Good. Well, on that understanding I'll be quite frank with you, Mi-chan."

Mie felt herself beginning to blush again. Kisses and caresses were one thing, but his use of the affectionate diminutive form of her given name was a greater intimacy which made her heart thump disturbingly.

"We realised that we couldn't keep it quiet for very long. Although we were actually enquiring into the incident after the press conference, the mere fact that Hara and I were interviewing people at all must have made it obvious that something was badly wrong. And of course we knew when I spoke to you all that Wilberforce had been killed, but it suited us to let a lot of gossip and speculation build up. Only Terry Phipps knew last night, and he was so upset that he had to be given a sedative. . . he's staying with one of the British consular staff for a day or two."

Kimura brought Mie her drink and after sitting down again beside her picked up his own for the first time and sipped. "Still, although I don't see how Phipps could have been in touch with any of the others, I'm not in the least surprised to hear that the word had got round the Tamahimeden by today that Wilberforce didn't in fact die a natural death."

"And what a horrible way to do it. Ugh!" Mie shuddered as Kimura sat very still, his glass poised in mid-air.

"Ah. Kuniko Doi told you, did she?"

"No, it was Erika. She's one of the models from Tokyo. I was talking to her for a few minutes while I was waiting to go to Kuniko Doi's room to interview her."

137

"One of the *models*? How in the world did she know?"

"What? Oh, I never asked. I suppose somebody else told her."

Kimura sighed. Hara's idea had seemed a good one at the time, but Mie's reaction confirmed the suspicion which had formed in his mind during the afternoon, that the murderer had been too smart for them. A word here, a word there was all it would have taken in that hothouse of gossip to ensure that everybody knew within a very short space of time the details Hara and he had gone to such pains to keep secret, without anyone being able to recall who had first divulged them. It was maddening. Infuriating, in fact.

"I suppose so," he said gruffly. "Well, how *was* Wesley Wilberforce killed, then? According to this Erika, I mean?" It was a long shot, but he had to be sure.

Mie looked at him in surprise. "You already know, so I can't see why you want me to tell you."

All at once Kimura became aware of an almost ungovernable fury bubbling up in him, directed partly at Mie and partly at himself for wasting so much time with her. He twisted round on the sofa, grabbed her by the upper arms and shook her, more violently than he intended to. "I said *according to Erika*," he shouted, temporarily blind to the fear in her startled eyes. "Why don't you just answer my question?"

Then he thrust her away from him and she fell back against the cushions, breathing heavily and rubbing her arms where he had gripped them. Kimura's fury began to subside almost as quickly as it had arisen, and he began to mutter apologies. For a few seconds neither of them moved or spoke, but then Kimura felt Mie's hand timidly creep into his.

"I'm sorry I made you angry," she whispered. "Erika said that he. . . that his head had been smashed in with a heavy table lamp. It must have been awful for poor Phipps-san to have to look at him after he was dead."

Kimura sat up and stared at her gratefully. Mie's colour was still high, her eyes were glistening and her lips were trembling adorably. Later he wasn't quite sure who took the initiative,

138

but the fact was that within seconds she was sprawled across him awkwardly, her warm, velvety mouth on his. Kimura found the next few minutes most agreeable, and sufficiently demanding of his attention to empty his mind almost completely of official concerns.

They marched back into his consciousness unbidden when Mie broke off the fourth or fifth delicious encounter of their lips and tongues, wriggled round in his arms to facilitate his unbuttoning of her blouse and, this achieved, moaned "*Mata kisu, hayaku kisu nasai*". Her words recalled to him their more peremptory English equivalent "Kiss me, damn you!", and the image of Selena with her arms snaking round his neck just two nights previously became superimposed on the flaming cheeks and squirming body of the eager girl on the sofa with him.

It was then that the telephone rang, and Kimura learned from the headquarters duty officer that the traffic police had reported a serious accident involving a foreigner: a woman identified from the passport and credit cards in her handbag as Selena Stoke-Lacy.

Chapter XVIII

"I can only repeat what I told you when the accident happened to Watanabe-san in the first place," Hiroshi Uehara said dully, "I believe that it was planned as a kind of warning to us – giving us a last chance to pay even after the deadline – showing us what they could do if we didn't cooperate. I can't believe that it was intended that anyone would be seriously hurt, let alone die from the injuries."

"So you say. And you also insist that following that incident you and Yasuda-san didn't change your minds about paying up."

Uehara's eyes flickered towards Hara who was sitting to one side of the manager's desk, across which Kimura faced him. "Yes, I do. I told Inspector Hara that yesterday. So we were naturally afraid that something else might happen, but –"

"But what?"

At Kimura's curt interruption Uehara raised his head sharply, with a momentary return to what was in more normal

140

times his habitual ease and authority of manner. "I'm trying to be helpful, Inspector, in the face of your wholly unnecessary insinuations to the contrary. What I was about to say is that in spite of that I still find it impossible to understand why anyone should wish to kill Wesley Wilberforce, of all people. It's all hopelessly confusing, and as for this accident to the lady journalist, Miss Stoke-Lacy. . . I'm convinced that *must* be just a very unlucky coincidence."

"It won't do, Uehara."

Otani stifled a yawn and shifted slightly in his seat in the corner of the room as he looked from Uehara's sallow face with its sheen of sweat to Kimura's, implacably inquisitorial now that he was well into his stride. It was still only ten minutes to ten in the morning, but Otani felt as if he had already done the better part of a day's work; on being told of the death of Yutaka Watanabe in hospital a little over twelve hours previously, he had instrtucted the duty officer to locate and summon Kimura, Hara, Noguchi and Junko Migishima to his office for a conference at seven-thirty.

It was not until then that he had learned from a wan and twitchy Kimura that Selena Stoke-Lacy had been run over by an unidentified car just outside the grounds of the Tamahimeden shortly before eight the previous evening and had been taken to the same hospital suffering from a broken leg, collarbone and several ribs. The five-o'clock fashion show had ended soon after six-thirty and the models had been out of their high-fashion clothes and into their jeans and T-shirts and away with their heavy stage make-up still intact almost before the people who had paid large sums of money to gaze at them had drifted out of the building. Over an hour later there were few people about and no witnesses to the accident had come forward.

The question why the English journalist was still in the vicinity so long after she had any obvious reason to be was just one of those Otani had instructed Kimura to ask her when he went to see her after Uehara had been interviewed. The Mode International affair was becoming more and more

141

complicated; getting out of hand was indeed the way he had described it during their early-morning conference which had ended with his having a private word with Junko Migishima before she went off to act out her role once more in the dressing-room. It was essential to make a fresh start, and this time Otani wanted to be fully informed. That was why he had elected to sit in, an anonymous, unidentified man in an unobtrusive suit, on the shaking-down of Hiroshi Uehara.

"It won't do because we're not fools, as I suspect you're at last beginning to realise. You don't look very well, Uehara, and you might just as well get down off your high horse, because let me assure you that you'll be feeling a lot worse before long if you go on withholding information from us."

"Would you like a cup of coffee, Uehara-san?" In spite of his bulk Inspector Hara was ideally cast in the contrasting "soft man" role they had agreed he should assume for the occasion. "All this must have come as something of a shock to you."

"Never mind coffee," Kimura snapped. "This man has a few things to tell us first." In accordance with the agreed outline script, Hara looked slightly hurt but subsided into his chair.

Kimura had no objection to being the hard man. In fact, bullying Uehara helped a little to soothe the rawness of his nerves over the frustrating anticlimax in his flat the previous evening after he had reluctantly disengaged himself from Mie's arms to answer the telephone. The duty officer was formal and ponderous in manner and would not be hurried in his stately account of what seemed to have happened to Selena Stoke-Lacy; would not indeed say whether she was alive or dead until he reached what he evidently considered to be the appropriate point in his narrative.

The call had taken so long that Kimura knew he could hardly blame Mie for the cooling of her ardour and her subsequent embarrassment and anger. It had been maddening to have to stand there helpless and watch her do up her blouse, then after a while disappear into his bathroom while

142

the man in the duty room waffled on; and little short of tragic to see her emerge again looking coldly composed, put on her coat, pick up her handbag, bow politely and let herself out. The door had clicked shut behind her just as Kimura finally learned that Selena's injuries, though extensive, were not thought to be such as to endanger her life.

"We're going right back to the beginning, Uehara. Whose idea was Mode International in the first place?" Uehara looked slightly vacant for a moment. "Come on, come on! We haven't got all day –"

"I seem to have some recollection of reading or hearing about similar shows in Japan before," Hara put in gently, and Uehara shot a grateful glance in his direction.

"Yes. It's not a new idea," he began thickly, then paused to clear his throat. "There have been a good many in Tokyo over the past ten years. 'Best Six' they were called. Staged at the Hanae Mori building, and always very successful. . . I mean we heard that even though they were very expensive to put on they paid their way and of course the publicity must have been worth a fortune to the Mori organisation."

"So you decided to exploit Hanae Mori's idea," Kimura said contemptuously. "Well, how long ago?"

Otani noticed that Uehara no longer looked at Kimura when he spoke, but addressed himself exclusively to Hara, who was nodding sympathetically.

"It's absurd to put it like that," he protested. "It's not a question of 'exploiting' anything or anybody. The whole fashion business is about publicity, and when one house gets hold of a good idea of course others think about ways of taking it up and adapting it for their own purposes. Just within the past couple of years we've got together with our competitors to form the Japan Designers' Council and stage regular joint shows in Tokyo. Bringing in foreign participants isn't all that different, although it is a lot more complicated and expensive. All the same, playing up the huge success of Japanese designers on the international scene makes long-term commercial sense for us, and the foreign designers we

143

approached jumped at the chance of showing part of their collections alongside ours. Particularly as so many of their clothes are marketed here in department stores under licence."

"Quite so," Hara murmured. "And Madame Yasuda is of course at the very summit of the profession. . . thanks I imagine very significantly to your own managerial skills."

Uehara looked at him sharply as though suspecting for a moment that he was being mocked, but there was nothing but sympathetic interest in Hara's mild eyes.

Kimura sneered. "That's a laugh. Everybody in this room knows Masako Yasuda managed her way to a fortune while Uehara here was still at high school. All the same, what happens to her now Watanabe's dead? What do you think, Uehara? She can't be any too pleased about the way things have turned out. I imagine the Wakamatsu board of directors will put their lawyers on to getting her out of their hair the moment they get back from trying to look solemn at their late unlamented chairman's funeral."

Otani tried to catch Kimura's eye. He was doing well but pushing ahead a little too fast. Fortunately Hara once more contributed a deft touch to the tiller.

"It is of course the international dimension of the House of Yasuda's interests which concerns you rather more than the domestic retailing side. I know my colleague realises that, Uehara-san. Though I'm equally sure you will appreciate that Madame Yasuda's business and – ah – former personal association with the late Yutaka Watanabe is something which can hardly be overlooked in the circumstances. No, please." Hara raised a hand as Uehara seemed to be about to say something. "We'll turn to that a little later, if you'll bear with us. You were, I believe, about to explain how long ago the idea of promoting an international fashion show along the lines of the Hanae Mori 'Best Six' projects was mooted? Oh, and I think we should all be interested to know how you arrived at the choice of Kobe as the ideal venue?"

When he had finished speaking Hara smiled deprecatingly,

144

gave a little sigh and politely cocked his head, like a kindly but slightly deaf academic trying to bring out the best in a *viva voce* candidate who was doing himself less than justice.

It seemed to Otani that Uehara had to some extent relaxed, even though his forehead still glistened and he glanced surreptitiously at his watch. "Well, I really can't see. . ."

The movement Kimura made was almost imperceptible, but it was enough to make Uehara begin again. "Very well, if you insist. We had been talking in general terms about the idea of staging our own international invitation show for a year or so before any firm decision was made to go ahead. My own original preference – just because of the new pattern of regular joint shows of Japanese designers' collections in Tokyo – was to do it in Paris, and although Madame Yasuda wasn't wholly persuaded we did get in touch with Tsutomu Kubota."

Hara nodded sagely. "His collaboration would have been essential, I suppose."

"Kubota or one of the other Paris-based Japanese designers would have had to undertake the local arrangements, yes. Madame Yasuda has known Kubota personally for a number of years and admires his work, so he was the first choice. I went to see him at her suggestion, and. . . well, quite frankly it soon became clear that if it were to be done in Paris at all it would mean working on Kubota's terms. In other words, it would become his show, not ours. We therefore decided to stage it here in Japan after all, and to go ahead quickly before Kubota decided to use the idea himself."

Uehara hesitated and fidgeted in his seat. "This is confidential, by the way –"

"Uehara! Two people have been murdered and another one seriously injured, and you blather about confidentiality? Get on with it!" Kimura was thoroughly into his role, and the righteousness of his indignation added colour to his performance. When Uehara continued his manner was again subdued.

"It seemed obvious that a good way to keep Kubota

145

friendly after turning down his proposals for Paris would be to invite him here as one of the participating designers. We also decided that we would choose a venue outside Tokyo, to avoid upsetting both the Japan Designers' Council and the Hanae Mori organisation, but wanted the show to be in a city with a strong international atmosphere." He shrugged. "And of course in effect that meant either Yokohama or Kobe, and Yokohama is so close to Tokyo that people wouldn't really get the point. Kobe, on the other hand, is over three hundred miles away, has excellent facilities and a sophisticated, cosmopolitan population. It was Madame Yasuda who remembered that Kobe is also Kubota's home town, and so we could represent the choice as a delicate compliment to him. It worked, and he was so flattered that he accepted right away. This was just under a year ago, and from that moment we pushed ahead with the detailed plans."

"I really think we might have that coffee now, Inspector Kimura." Hara said. "Don't you?"

Kimura nodded, picked up the telephone on the manager's desk and spoke to the secretary in the outer office. It was all taking a long time, but Otani was well pleased with the way things were going, and from behind Uehara's back nodded approvingly to Kimura and Hara, both of whom could see him. The atmosphere in the room was perceptibly more relaxed, and when Kimura next spoke his tone was less belligerent.

"It'll be here in a few minutes. All right, Uehara. That makes sense. And it accounts for Kubota being in on it. What about the others, though? Jean-Claud Villon, Marian Norton and Wesley Wilberforce? How did they get chosen? Did you approach any others apart from them?"

"We tried to get Valentino or Versace but neither was interested and Madame Yasuda wasn't keen on any of the other leading Italians. We wanted at least one woman among the foreign designers and thought about Jean Muir, but she had taken part in Hanae Mori's 'Best Six' shows. It seems Marian Norton was very friendly and cooperative when

146

Madame Yasuda spent some months in New York about seven or eight years ago –"

"This was before you joined the House of Yasuda, was it?" Probably because he had not previously uttered a word, Otani's quiet interjection had a dramatic effect, and he noticed that Uehara literally jumped in his seat before swivelling round to look at him.

"Yes. It was."

"Thank you."

If Kimura and Hara had to be thrown off their stride that was as good a moment as any for it to happen, because as Otani nodded politely and prepared to sink back into his former inconspicuous role as part of the furniture somebody knocked at the door, and then immediately opened it. It was the manager's secretary, with a tray. Kimura just managed to stop himself from thanking her with the fulsome charm he directed almost automatically at any presentable woman of any age. Instead he frowned sternly at Uehara while she apologised for the intrusion and poured out their coffee from a vacuum jug which the speed of her response suggested had been ready and waiting in the outer office for some time.

Their refreshments distributed, and the little packets of coffee whitener and sugar duly emptied into the cups, Kimura caught Otani's eye. In response to the interrogative tilt of Kimura's eyebrow Otani shook his head almost impercep-tibly and indicated Hara with a movement of one finger. Hara did not appear to be looking at him at the time, but responded without hesitation.

"Do help yourself to a biscuit, Uehara-san," he said hospitably, "then we'll just tie up these loose ends. I'm personally interested by the fact that in spite of having invited Tsutomu Kubota you also brought Jean-Claud Villon from France. I suppose although Kubota has made his reputation in Paris he's neverthless still regarded essentially as a Japanese designer, unlike some others. . .Yuki, say. After all, Yuki designed for Mrs Margaret Thatcher, I believe?"

Uehara seemed quite surprised by this further evidence of

147

Hara's familiarity with the world of fashion. "Yes, that's so. But there was another reason for inviting Jean-Claud Villon. The Wakamatsu department stores have the exclusive agency for his menswear and accessories. They complement the House of Yasuda's *prêt-à-porter* clothes and the other lines retailed through our boutiques."

"Of course. I remember seeing his name in advertisements," Hara lied smoothly. "And wasn't there some link of a similar kind with Wesley Wilberforce?"

Uehara seemed to be having some difficulty with the plastic wrapper of his second biscuit. "There's been some talk about one, but nothing has come of it so far, and now of course. . ." He looked up after he finally managed to tear it open. "I myself was very keen to invite Bruce Oldfield from England. He's young, he designs for Princess Diana and he's in the news a lot. However, I was overruled."

"I see. And the choice fell on Wesley Wilberforce. He was Madame Yasuda's preference, I presume."

Uehara turned towards Kimura, who was dabbing the corner of his mouth delicately with a snowy handkerchief and hastily glared at him. "Yes, he was," he said. "His work is rather conservative, like Madame Yasuda's. And of course they studied with Coco Chanel in Paris at the same time, years ago."

Chapter XIX

"Only tomorrow left," Erika murmured as Junko Migishima pulled up the zipper for her and fastened the hook and eye at the top of the Jean-Claud Villon dress she was to wear first. "She's going to miss all this flesh. Look, she can hardly keep her hands off her."

The second of the day's three shows was due to begin in fifteen minutes, and on the other side of the big room Kuniko Doi was watching intently as Vanessa Radley stepped out of her jeans, flung them over the back of a chair and then began to ease a pair of tights on to her long, slender legs. This done she put on the court shoes one of the dressers passed to her, then pulled off her sweatshirt and stood there with negligent grace naked to the waist until the dresser eased one of Jean-Claude Villon's froths of chiffon carefully over her head. Kuniko Doi smiled and said something to the English girl but Junko and Erika were too far away to hear what it was. "Doi-san does have a reputation to keep up, after all," Junko said. "Vanessa-san doesn't seem to be paying much attention, though."

149

Junko was herself by now quite adjusted to the casual attitude to semi-nudity shown by all the models, but remained interested by the foreign girls' bodies and envious of the length and straightness of their legs. She was unselfish enough to admit to herself that the Japanese models were quite impressive in that department too. Junko understood only a few English phrases and could speak less, so communication with Vanessa Radley and Barbi Mingus was tricky, but during the few days of hectic activity they had all spent in each other's company she had got to know most of the others quite well.

It was always particularly pleasant to talk to Erika, and not only because her Japanese was so fluent. Erika was always friendly and relaxed, and she had an amused eye for the extravagances and pretensions of some of her colleagues. Moreover, although Junko's services were theoretically available to everybody, Erika and one or two of the other girls had soon established priority claims on her help, and the harassed dressing-room supervisor had made no objection. Junko had also lent a hand now and then to the experts she had learned to refer to as the stylist and the hair-make, but always melted away discreetly when one of the designers put in an appearance to fuss and worry over a particular creation. At this moment it was the calm before the storm, with nobody clamouring for her and there was time for an unobtrusive minute or two of chat with the ideal person for Junko's immediate purposes.

"I do feel sorry for Vanessa, all the same," Erika said thoughtfully. "With such an awful thing happening and nobody to talk to, really. I think it's quite brave of her to carry on, especially now that Terry Phipps is in such trouble."

"Terry Phipps? What trouble?" It was a good opening, and Junko kept her tone as light and casual as possible.

"Oh, come on, Junko. You must have heard all the scandal. Why do you think we haven't seen Terry here since they found Wesley Wilberforce's body? The rumour is that he's been arrested."

150

"What? Who says so?"

Erika waved a hand airily and absent-mindedly proffered a cheek to be kissed by Gene, her male colleague from Tokyo who with his partner enjoyed a longer break between shows than the girls because they had much less to do, and now breezed past them. "Who? Oh, everybody I've spoken to."

"There's been nothing like that in the papers," Junko protested stoutly. "If it comes to that, one of the Japanese girls said he's gone back to England, but I don't believe that either."

There was no reason why Junko should, since she had heard no less an authority than "Gorgeous" Kimura that morning assure Superintendent Otani that the Ministry of Justice had instructed the immigration staff at all ports of departure to withhold exit clearance for Phipps and the other visiting foreign-passport holders until further notice. Phipps himself was still in custody but would probably be allowed to move back to his hotel in Kobe later that day. "You don't really think he did it, do you Erika-san?" she added as the other girl shrugged.

Instead of answering immediately, Erika glanced again across the busy room to where Kuniko Doi was still talking to Vanessa Radley, one jewelled claw now lightly grasping the girl's forearm. "Still trying hard," she said, then turned her startling blue eyes back to Junko. "Well, I can't think who else it might have been," she said. "Before it happened Terry was forever going on about how fed up he was with Wesley. At the time it seemed sort of pathetic and funny at the same time. Two elderly gays squabbling with each other, especially when Wesley tried so hard all the time to look pompous and respectable. Love's a strange thing, but it's hard to imagine that Terry might have had it in him to commit murder."

"That's what I think, too," Junko said, "especially like that –"

"Like what? Has somebody at last discovered what actually *happened* to Wesley?"

Junko was both startled and pleased to discover Tsutomu Kubota at her elbow. She had hardly hoped to catch two fluent speakers of both Japanese and English at the same time. "Hello, Stom," the Swedish girl said, accepting another kiss on the cheek. Although tense, Junko found time to wonder whether she could ever learn to cope with seemingly countless embraces during a working day in so matter-of-fact a way. On the whole she thought she would rather enjoy it. . . both Gene and Kubota were attractive men in their very different ways. She waited to be quizzed further by Kubota, but in spite of his having used Japanese Erika chattered away in incomprehensible English for a sentence or two before turning back to Junko and reverting to Japanese.

"Oh no, look, there's that girl from the *Kobe Shimbun* again over there. She's beginning to haunt this place, but I'm not surprised. The media are having the time of their lives. You'd better give her an interview like all the rest of us if you really know something we don't."

Suddenly her hand flew to her lips and her eyes widened. "Junko! You didn't mean it surely? I mean, you didn't. . .*see* anything, did you?"

"No, no. I. . . that is. . . oh, please excuse me. I must go, the hair-make's calling for me."

It was done, and Junko fled leaving Erika and Kubota together. During the following chaotic hour and a half she had no further opportunity to make conversation, and certainly no desire to speak to Mie Nakazato, who was now hovering uncertainly in Kuniko Doi's vicinity. With luck she might not have to set any more balls rolling anyway, though the more Junko thought about what she had done, the more the ideas and images tumbling about crazily in her mind terrified her. She nevertheless managed to go about her work with much of her usual unobtrusiveness while trying to keep a particular eye on Vanessa Radley.

It was true; the English girl was being brave. She was obviously a professional who took her work seriously, but even though that afternoon she was never less than several yards away from her it was not difficult for Junko to see the strain and unhappiness in her face every time she returned to the dressing-room to change. Indeed, she was struck by the way Vanessa seemed to put on and take off an expression of glazed hauteur with each different ensemble, her true face when exposed between times seeming as timidly vulnerable as her childish little breasts and bony hips.

People did seem to go out of their way to be nice to her. Although she and Barbi Mingus were the protégées of particular designers, they, like all the others, modelled the clothes of all the participants during the course of the show. Although it was only at the gala preview that all the designers had been expected to make a personal appearance, Masako Yasuda, Marian Norton, Tsutomu Kubota and Jean-Claud Villon had all looked in at least once during the course of the first full day's programme, and on reflection Junko recalled that they had each seemed to make a point of talking to Vanessa.

So far that day Jean-Claud Villon had spent some time in the dressing-room during the first show, mainly badgering the stylist, but also going over to Vanessa and even removing the smouldering Gauloise cigarette dangling from his lower lip in defiance of the "No Smoking" signs in order to nuzzle briefly at her neck and exchange a few words with her. Now, with the second show nearly over, Kubota had also spent a few minutes in the English girl's company and seemed to be at something of a loose end, as indeed did Marian Norton who had arrived about half-way through and personally supervised the process when Vanessa changed into one of her own ensembles.

Then it was the finale with all the models on stage. The stylist and the hair-make had disappeared for their break with their respective assistants, and though the music of the show was clearly audible and there were still at least half a dozen people left in the big room it seemed strangely empty. It was also relatively tidy, since most of the clothes were now back on their hangers protected by plastic covers and arranged on

153

rails in readiness for the last show of the day. Even so, Junko tripped up as she moved in front of Kubota and Marian Norton and almost dropped the dress she was carrying. The American woman saved the day by grabbing Junko's arm, and Junko babbled profuse apologies as she recovered her balance, sharply aware of the intensity of Marian Norton's scrutiny. The huge eyes in the pale, cadaverous face with its weird, dramatic make-up seemed to consume her, and Junko had no need to simulate a mixture of embarrassment and alarm and shake her head uncomprehendingly when the designer said something to her in English. She had not heard Marian Norton's speaking voice at close quarters before, and found its deep, husky quality disturbing.

"Norton-san was asking you whether it's true you know how Wesley Wilberforce was killed," Kubota said quietly. The sound of the comfortable accent of the Kobe area in which Junko had been born and lived all her life came as a relief, even though Kubota's manner was alien, almost like that of a foreigner, she thought. "You were called away while we were with Erika before the show."

"Yes. I'm sorry," Junko said with what she hoped was suitable humility, feeling rather than seeing Marian Norton's witch-like eyes still on her.

"Well? Do you?" Kubota's voice had taken on a certain edge, and Junko was no longer quite so sure that she would enjoy being kissed by him, even on the cheek. "Do you or do you not know how Wesley Wilberforce was killed?"

Suddenly he smiled at Junko, who was still clutching the dress she had been about to hang on its rail. "I'm sorry if I sounded impatient. It's just that none of us – his old friends – know, you see, and we're naturally a little upset at being kept in the dark. . . it makes one imagine all kinds of awful possibilities. Of course, you may have just heard one of the wild rumours going around."

Junko shook her head firmly. "Oh, no," she said. "It's not a rumour, but. . . I'm very sorry, I was told not to discuss it with anybody, you see. Not with anybody at all."

Kubota turned to the American woman at his side and spoke to her rapidly in English while she held her unfathomable gaze on Junko. When he paused she asked him a question, still without looking at him, and then Kubota addressed himself to Junko again. "Who told you? The police, you mean? You've been questioned by the police?"

Junko nodded, wide-eyed. "So, please excuse me. I have my work to do," she muttered, then ducked in a sort of bow and turned away, but Marian Norton shot out a thin hand discoloured with brown spots and blotches and seized Junko by the arm. Her grip was almost painfully strong.

"Just a moment. What is your name, dear?" she said hollowly.

The two English phrases she used were among the very few Junko actually understood. "My name is Junko Migishima," she said haltingly, suppressing a powerful urge to free herself with the greatest of ease and subject the woman in return to a brief exhibition of some of the more disagreeable consequences of tangling with a black belt *aikido* expert.

"You *do* speak English, then?"

"I not speak English," Junko replied truthfully, and relapsed into Japanese as she turned her head to look at Kubota. "Please ask Norton-san to let go of my arm," she said. "She's hurting me. And the show's over, they're coming back, and I have many things to do or I shall get into trouble. The supervisor's already looking upset."

There was indeed plenty to do as the girls and the two male models rampaged back into the dressing-room stripping themselves while still on the move and followed by Kuniko Doi. The TV star had never once, after any of the shows so far completed, gone to her private accommodation to change before first hanging about in the main dressing-room until the last pairs of lissom legs and pert breasts had disappeared from view under the inevitable jeans and sweatshirts. All Junko had to do now was bustle about putting things away, so she had plenty of opportunities to notice Kubota cross the room unobtrusively and have a brief conversation with Kuniko

155

Doi, and also Marian Norton standing stock-still as people ebbed and flowed around her, gazing pensively in her direction but never quite catching her eye.

Chapter XX

"I don't like it," Noguchi said, lowering his close-cropped head and swaying it from side to side like a bull in a ring. "I've got responsibilities for that kid."

Otani went over to the window and stood beside his old friend, staring with him towards the lofty cranes of Kobe Harbour, clearly visible over the roofline in the last of the daylight. Earlier the screaming of the wheeling gulls had been audible in his office even over the constant rumble of the traffic outside, but they had disappeared during the course of the afternoon. "I know you have, Ninja," he said. "That's why I told you what I had in mind. I'm sorry. To be quite honest with you, my wife wanted to volunteer herself for the job –"

"Out of the question!" From being worried and upset, Noguchi now sounded as if he had become positively angry.

"I know. That's what I told her. I very much doubt whether anybody other than Hara even noticed her go out of the room before the end of that preview, still less anybody who knew her."

157

"Except Chummy, maybe. You keep the wife well out of all this."

Otani sighed and nodded. "Yes. There is a faint chance of that, I suppose. I prefer not to think about it. In any case it would have been totally impracticable, whereas Junko-san's already in place. Look, Ninja, I'm sorry about this too. I know how you must feel."

Otani cast a sideways look at Noguchi's scowling face and momentarily saw him again in his mind's eye shuffling along red-faced in an agony of embarrassment in his hired, ludicrously ill-fitting morning suit on the Migishimas' wedding day. As the solemn little procession moved towards the top table at the wedding he and Hanae had applauded furiously and glared round at the other guests, daring anyone to snigger. Then he remembered the clumsy sincerity of Noguchi's speech as the couple's formal go-between, and the simple effectiveness of his words, and cleared his throat uncomfortably. The responsibilities of the go-between in a Japanese marriage do not end on the wedding day, and Noguchi still kept a jealously protective eye not only on Junko but also on her large, beefy and devoted husband.

"She's a very resourceful girl, though, and she's proved she knows how to handle this sort of situation. Look how extraordinarily well she did with that boat-load of gangsters in the Inland Sea while I was in England."

Otani was taken aback by the vehemence of Noguchi's response as the older man swung and grasped him by the lapel. "Yes, she did, and no thanks to that selfish prick Kimura. I tell you, I damn nearly killed him when I found out he'd pushed her into it." Otani gently detached Noguchi's hand, drew back a little and then smiled distantly, subtly reasserting his authority. "I can well believe it, even though you know perfectly well that's not quite how it happened, Ninja. I had a very long talk with her after I got back and read the reports. Anyway, that's all past history now, and I'm sure that, having got an 'exceptional merit' promotion out of it, Junko-san has no regrets. And you must simply take my word for it that there was no question this morning of my pushing her into this new gambit. Quite the reverse. I fancy she'd been rather fed up when Hara took her off investigating some bogus priest or other to put her in the Tamahimeden. When I raised my idea with her she was very positive, very enthusiastic, saw it as a challenge to her skills as an actress, I think. And we'll take good care of her, Ninja. She'll come to no harm, I promise you. Now, we're agreed on what you're to tell Kubota?"

Noguchi sighed heavily but said nothing, and after a while Otani moved away and went to stand behind his desk, where he riffled through a small pile of papers. "We gave Uehara a grilling later on over there. At least, Hara and Kimura did and I listened in. He's an intelligent man and probably holding quite a lot back. All the same, I'm inclined to think he was as taken in by the phony extortion bid as somebody hoped we would be, and if I'm right that alters the picture very significantly. Something else almost as important emerged, as well."

"Which was?"

Otani suppressed a smile at Noguchi's question, relieved that he seemed to be accepting, however reluctantly, the necessity to use Junko Migishima as bait. "Which was that all four of the visiting designers were in effect personally selected by Masako Yasuda."

"Big deal," Noguchi commented, still with his back to Otani. Then he slowly turned and faced him. "Obviously they were. What else did you expect?"

Otani nodded in qualified acknowledgement of his point. "I realise it must sound trite, but hear me out – you weren't there and I was. What came over to me while Uehara was talking was that she'd rather cleverly made it *seem* – even or perhaps especially to him, her right-hand man – that the project developed quite naturally out of purely commercial considerations. The idea of staging Mode International at all, of choosing Kobe as the venue, and above all of bringing Kubota, plus the Frenchman, the American woman and that poor fellow Wilberforce together here at the same time. Yasuda used Uehara very subtly, going along with his ideas and suggestions up to a point but always managing to frustrate them where they deviated from her own plans. And when she did that she usually managed to make it seem as if it was just force of circumstances that made it necessary to do the thing her way rather than his. I honestly believe he had no idea she'd led him by the nose – at least until this morning. By now I suppose he might have realised what we were driving at and maybe even begun to put two and two together."

"You sure?"

"About my interpretation of what happened? No, of course not. And I haven't tried it on Hara or Kimura yet. But they didn't get anything significant out of any of the other people they questioned and I can't think of a better hypothesis at the moment. Come and sit down, Ninja. Yes, I know we've both got things to do, but they need thinking about, and two heads are better than one." As he slumped into his familiar chair Otani glanced at the clock over the filing cabinet against the wall.

"Ten past five. The third show should be under way by now. We don't have a lot of time, Ninja. Only tonight and tomorrow, in effect. We can hardly keep them all together here after that, and the district prosecutor made it very clear when I spoke to him on the phone this afternoon that he's not about to agree to our arresting the lot of them on suspicion. Wouldn't even if they were all Japanese, let alone famous and wealthy foreigners. At least, my wife tells me they're famous and the papers and the TV seem to think they are."

He leant forward with an air of urgent anxiety. "I had to do something, Ninja. We've held the media off with some success for a couple of days, but they're all asking questions, and you know as well as I do that the weekly magazines must be prepared to pay an informant good money for the details. I can't believe they won't get at somebody working at the mortuary before long."

He picked up a copy of the lurid tabloid *Kansai Sport* and tossed it over to Noguchi.

160

"This evening's. I picked it up an hour ago on my way back to headquarters. Half way down the page – 'Mystery At The Morgue', it says. And they've got Watanabe's death and a not-so-subtle hint that we're not releasing details of the Wilberforce killing because the two are linked. *And* a little piece about the English fashion writer being run over. Not surprising that they've run what passes for a leading article all about the tragedy stalking the ill-fated Mode International. Same page as the porno short story and the comic strips. You can bet the *Kobe Shimbun* will have it in the morning, a bit less obviously no doubt."

"All right," Noguchi said after a cursory look at the paper. "Made your point."

"Sorry. I don't want to labour it. Anyway, by now I'm sure Junko-san will have stirred things up a bit. Uehara too, probably, because towards the end of the session Hara did a nice job of implying that somebody working backstage had admitted seeing something or someone at the time the Englishman was murdered but was holding out on us. Judging by what I've heard about these fashion people, it'll be all round the place in no time."

"Any theory about why Yasuda should want Wilberforce done in?"

Otani shook his head. "No. I haven't got that far yet. Or perhaps I should say I've got three or four theories, but none I'd put money on. For the moment I'd be pleased to get solid confirmation that I'm right in believing that Masako Yasuda organised this whole Mode International set-up with the primary purpose of assembling four other people from three different countries in Kobe at this time. And what's more, that she began doing so as long as a year ago."

Noguchi's shrewd blackcurrant eyes flickered again over the newspaper he still held in his hand before he threw it on the floor beside his chair. "That would have been before the Wakamatsu directors started gunning for her boy friend Watanabe," he said thoughtfully. "Right?"

Otani shook his head. "No, I don't think so, and that's the

161

interesting point. We'll have to pin Uehara down more precisely on dates, and perhaps later on ask the Met to go through the relevant files at the House of Yasuda headquarters in Tokyo. If and when it comes to proving something, that is. But as far as I've been able to find out it seems to have been at about the same time." He paused and rubbed his hands together. It was getting dark outside and the big room had become chilly in spite of the fact that the antiquated central heating system was burbling and thumping to itself. He recalled that there should be an electric fan heater knocking about in a cupboard somewhere and resolved to ask somebody to look it out for him the following day.

"I dropped in on a fellow Rotarian this afternoon," he continued as Noguchi stared at him expressionlessly, his eyelids half closed. "By way of being a friend of mine. He's vice-president of the chamber of commerce, due to become chairman next year. It's automatic. He's also high up in the Takashimaya department store chain – deadly rivals of the Wakamatsu people, of course,"

Noguchi fumbled in his pocket and found a toothpick. Otani was pleasantly surprised to notice that it was a new one, still in its individual paper wrapper.

"Gave you some useful dirt, did he?" Noguchi mumbled as he dug between two of his few remaining teeth.

"Yes, you could put it like that. He keeps a confidential personal file on Watanabe, has done for years, he told me. Ever since the Takashimaya people began to hear whispers to the effect that Watanabe was dipping his hand in the till at Wakamatsu and that his little arrangement with Masako Yasuda wasn't exactly square and above-board. What surprised my friend was that the other directors took so long to make up their minds to – excuse me, I'd better answer that."

Otani hauled himself out of his chair to answer the telephone and switched on the reading lamp on his desk as he identified himself and then listened attentively. The small pool of light was reflected upwards by the sheet of plate-glass which covered the entire surface of the ponderous, old-

162

fashioned desk and gave his face a sinister, menacing quality like that of somebody in a horror movie. The spectacle rather amused Noguchi, who glanced towards the light switches on the wall by the door and made a move as though about to get up and go and turn on the harsh, utilitarian overhead lighting, but then slumped back comfortably in the gloom.

"Really?" Otani said into the telephone after what seemed a very long time. "That's extremely interesting, Kimura-kun. And very good of them to pass the information on. I must admit I'm not quite sure where it leaves us, but I think we'd better get to work fast to double-check the alibis certain people provided you and Hara with, don't you? Yes, of course, I'll get a message to Hara right away. And you'd better get over to the hospital and get a proper statement from the lady if she's in a fit state to give one. Good. My respects to the Consul-General. I shall hope to see him at the opening of the bonsai exhibition on Saturday. Yes. Goodbye."

Otani replaced the receiver slowly. "Not that I can see much chance of being able to go myself at this rate," he added to Noguchi, and then himself went to the door and switched on the lights before returning to his easy-chair. When he did sit down it was only on the edge of the seat, to gaze thoughtfully at Noguchi who roused himself in response.

"That was Kimura, ringing from the British Consulate-General in Osaka. About the English woman journalist who was run over last night. Apparently he phoned the woman she's staying with here in Kobe when he heard the news last night. A cousin, it seems. Kimura knows her –" Otani paused abruptly, stopping himself just in time from referring to the case in which Mrs Byers-Pinkerton had figured a few years previously and which had involved personal tragedy for Noguchi. "But couldn't get any sense out of her about next-of-kin in England who should be informed. He had to notify the accident to the British consular people anyway, and they must have got on the telex to London right away. To cut a long story short, Kimura was called over there this

163

afternoon and told in confidence that according to their passport office records this lady was married to Tsutomu Kubota in London seven years ago and so far as they are aware, still is. What do you make of that, Ninja?" Twitching with nervous energy, Otani rose to his feet again and this time Noguchi followed suit.

"I'll tell Hara for you," he said, seemingly unsurprised by the news. "Got to talk to him anyway about Watanabe. The widow's due to arrive from Tokyo this evening to give her instructions. You were going to tell me what your Rotary pal had to tell you."

Otani looked at him blankly, his thoughts still dominated by Kimura's revelation. "Oh," he said after a while. "Mostly confirmation of what we'd already suspected, really. He had it on very reliable authority that the other directors *did* give Watanabe an ultimatum just about a year ago. He was either to get rid of the Yasuda boutiques somehow or other, or resign."

Chapter XXI

Junko Migishima peered at her reflection in the steamy mirror of the medicine cabinet as she put the finishing touches to her make-up. It was one of the minor points of contention between her and Migishima that even after more than three years of marriage she declined absolutely – except when occasional undercover duties demanded it – to adopt the normal uninspiring camouflage of the young married Japanese woman. Not that her husband had ever done more than hint in the most oblique way that they ought to "settle down", and then almost always after he had been to see his formidable mother or spoken to her on the telephone. On such occasions Junko had her own infallibly effective ways of handling him.

All the same, since being assigned to work at the Tamahimeden among professional models she had modified her appearance so as to appear businesslike yet unobtrusive. Having kept her eyes open and learned a few tricks of the cosmetician's trade over the past few days she was looking

165

forward to the morale-boosting effects of putting on full, improved war-paint for a while before having to play the drab, lonely and unhappy housewife again in order to catch Brother Yamanaka out and obtain indisputable evidence of the true nature of his idiosyncratic interpretation of the concept of Divine Possession.

Reasonably satisfied with the results of her efforts, Junko passed noiselessly out of the cramped bathroom in her stockinged feet and slipped into her coat, then checked her handbag and glanced round the small living-room before leaving, thinking as she did every day how lucky they were to have such a nice place of their own in which to live, even if the repayments for the huge loan they had taken out to acquire it did stretch out ahead of them for a period of years she could hardly envisage.

It was still only just after seven, and since the shoji screens were still in place and the kitchen and bathroom boasted only small reeded glass windows high up the wall, she had no idea what the weather was like outside. She had already placed a thermos jug of very hot water on the table beside the wrapped loaf of bread, the electric toaster and the jars of instant coffee, "Creap" powdered milk and Meidi-ya marmalade, and now on an afterthought fetched the half-used packet of Snow Brand butter from the tiny refrigerator in the kitchen and put it on a plate beside the other things. It was quite chilly enough in the room for it to stay firm until her husband was likely to surface and want his breakfast. He had not arrived home until after midnight, whispering, as he slipped under the warm futon and as Junko greeted him sleepily, that Kimura had – grudgingly, she was quite sure – told him he needn't report until ten-thirty that morning.

Junko looked at her watch and then tiptoed over to the sliding fusuma screen which divided the six-mat bedroom from the living-room and eased it open an inch or two. There was no movement from the shapeless heap of bedding on the tatami matting, so she merely smiled and left him to it, slipping into her shoes at the entrance to the flat and closing

166

the heavy metal door with exaggerated care behind her.

It proved to be a dull, misty morning, the outlines of the heavy trucks rumbling along the elevated expressway beside the Migishimas' apartment block softened and made mysterious, and the crumpled hills inland mere shadows in various intensities of grey. Not for the first time, Junko thought they looked exactly like mountains in a Chinese-style ink painting, and wondered why people often describe such paintings as impressionistic.

The nearest bus stop served two different routes to Sannomiya and she had only two or three minutes to wait with a handful of other people before one appeared out of the haze and she boarded it, taking the fare-stage slip which protruded at her from the dispenser inside the rear door like a rude little boy's tongue as her legs broke the beam of the electric eye by the step. At the front of the bus was an illuminated sign which informed passengers of the amount of money each must drop with the numbered slip onto the endless belt in the plastic box under the eye of the driver on leaving by the front door – unless, like Junko, they had a monthly season ticket. All good employers in Japan meet the commuting expenses of the people who work for them, and in the morning rush hour few passengers pay cash for their rides.

It was still only ten past eight by the time Junko arrived at the Tamahimeden, nearly two hours before she was supposed to report for duty, and she was pleased to see that everything seemed to be as she had expected following a chat she had had with one of the cleaning-women the previous day. The garrulous old soul had much enjoyed being drawn out so sympathetically about her rheumatism by such a nice, well-mannered young woman of the kind you didn't come across very often these days, and had said as much rather pointedly to the woman next door with the noisy children when she met her buying fish sausage in the covered neighbourhood market later, quite unaware that she had been expertly pumped about the routine arrangements for opening up the Tamahimeden each morning.

Junko knew that the night security man let the two cleaners in at eight, that one of them brought a morning paper in for him and that he then invariably made himself scarce and sat reading it over a cup of coffee he had made for himself in the basement restaurant until it was time to go up and hang about in the lobby and go off duty as soon as the first member of the office staff arrived shortly before nine. Meantime the women got on with their work.

When Junko reached the big glass doors she was at first disconcerted to discover that they did not open automatically for her, but was quickly relieved to discover that they were open by little more than a crack, having evidently been unlocked but left on manual control. It was in fact much quieter to slide one of them gently to one side barely enough to enable her to slip inside the deserted lobby and then nearly close it again that it would have been if they had rumbled open by themselves at her approach.

Junko guessed that the cleaners' first job would be to set the main salon to rights ready for the eleven o'clock show, and the past few days' experience suggested that it was highly unlikely that any of the Mode International people would put in an appearance much before ten. She therefore went first to the ground-floor office which had been placed at the disposal of the House of Yasuda.

The door was locked, but that was no problem. The internal locks at the Tamahimeden were simple affairs, not nearly as formidable as those in a modern hotel, and Inspector Hara had in any case lent Junko the master key he had obtained from the manager on the day Wilberforce had been murdered.

Junko let herself in, leaving the door ajar behind her, and crossed quickly to the desk, wrinkling her nose in distaste at the sour, stale smell of the previous day's cigarettes. It was even worse by the desk, on which stood an ashtray brimming over with bent butts, most of them apparently having been stubbed out after no more than a few puffs. They were evidence of nervousness on Uehara's part, but although

168

Junko had no very clear idea what she was looking for, she was definitely hoping for rather more than that.

She found it not in any of the drawers of the desk, nor by skimming through the folders of papers on its surface or on the smaller, folding table used by Kinjo following Uehara's arrival in Kobe. A cursory examination suggested that they were innocuous enough: simple working files relating to the costs of renting the Tamahimeden, receipts from sales of tickets, statements from agencies of fees due to the models, technical notes, press cuttings and so on. There seemed to be nothing in them in the way of correspondence either with the foreign designers or with Kuniko Doi's agent, but Junko was not surprised. It would have been fascinating to know how much they were paying Doi, but she assumed that such paperwork would be kept at the Yasuda offices in Tokyo anyway.

It was in an inside pocket of the ultra-smart and no doubt hideously expensive Italian jacket on a hanger suspended from a hook on the back of the door that Junko found what was evidently Uehara's personal diary. She had seen Uehara wearing the jacket when escorting particularly favoured visitors backstage between shows, and could well believe that he kept it in the office for this purpose and wore something more practical on the way to and from his hotel and while at his desk. It was nearly eight twenty-five and high time she was elsewhere, so Junko did no more than flip through the slender little leather-bound book in the pleasurable conviction that it would repay closer study, then pop it in her bag before taking a last look round the room.

The old woollen cardigan draped over the back of Kinjo's chair caught her eye and Junko quickly dipped a hand into each of its two shallow pockets. The left-hand one was empty, while the other contained nothing but a crumpled slip of paper she took at first for a receipt of some kind, until she smoothed it out and saw printed wording on it. Junko stood very still and missed a breath, then stuffed the paper into her bag with Uehara's diary, opened the door a crack and peeped cautiously out into the corridor.

169

Everything was still quiet outside as she closed and re-locked the door behind her and made her way quietly to the emergency stairs and up to the main floor. There she paused, swallowed twice to counter the dryness in her throat, and again surveyed the situation.

The doors of the main salon were propped wide open and she could hear the clatter of chairs and the voices of the cleaning-women from within. Reassured, Junko made her way soundlessly but without unnatural haste along the thickly carpeted corridor towards the main dressing-room where she quickly took off and hung up her coat and slipped into the smock she wore for her work. Then she looked indecisively for a moment at her handbag before taking Uehara's diary, the paper from Kinjo's cardigan and her Hyogo police identification card out of it. She smoothed out the paper again and slipped it into the diary, hauled up her skirt and tucked both diary and ID card into the top of her knickers, snug against her belly and held securely in place by her tights. She was wearing a full skirt anyway, and the loose smock over that added to her confidence. She put her purse openly in the pocket of her smock as all the staff routinely did, knowing that there was nothing in it which hinted at her true profession, nor remaining in the handbag which she left with her coat. Then she looked around the big room for a cleaning-rag of some kind, but had to make do with a feather duster she found in a corner, even though it was awkward to conceal under her smock.

Still unnoticed by the cleaners, Junko slipped into the cross-corridor in which the bridal changing-rooms were located, studied the name-cards on the doors and used the master key again to let herself into the room placed at the disposal of Masako Yasuda. It showed little sign of her having made much use of it, and indeed Junko had already reported to Inspector Hara that she herself had seen the designer only twice while at work in the dressing-room; once assembling with all the others apart from the murdered Wilberforce to appear on stage for the finale of the gala preview, and again late on the afternoon of the second full day.

170

There were two dresses protected by plastic covers hanging in the built-in wardrobe and two pairs of shoes on the rail beneath, while a half-used lipstick lay beside a box of tissues on the dressing-table alongside a copy of the programme for the show. Brandishing her feather duster as a mute explanation of her presence in the unlikely event of her being seen there, Junko moved over to the dressing-table and quickly looked into each of its four shallow drawers, all of which proved to be empty. It was still not quite twenty to nine, and she reflected that there was perhaps time to look around Marian Norton and Jean-Claud Villon's rooms before it would be prudent to return to the main dressing-room and busy herself innocently there as people began to arrive.

Junko moved to the door and looked cautiously out. The furtiveness was a bad mistake, she realised as she felt a lurching in her stomach and the adrenalin surge into her bloodstream. For she was no longer alone.

"You're very early," the new arrival said, sounding if anything gratified rather than angry or suspicious. "A lucky coincidence. I've been wanting to have a quiet word with you."

Chapter XXII

"No, I didn't see him this morning," Kimura said. "I came straight here. I think he was planning to go and see the district prosecutor, anyway. All I know is that he wants us to meet him here at the Tamahimeden at about six."

As always when thinking hard, Hara took off his glasses and cleaned them thoroughly, then blinked a great many times in rapid succession before replacing them. "Somewhat premature, surely? A meeting with the district prosecutor, I mean. Mr Akamatsu has something of a reputation for being. . ."

"Difficult to convince. Sure." Kimura grinned and stretched luxuriously in the Tamahimeden manager's chair as he looked up into Hara's pale, scholarly face. "I think you've probably got it the wrong way round, though. If I know anything about Akamatsu, he's called the chief over there to find out how far we've got. Now that Watanabe's gone to Hiroshima to buy tobacco –"

It was Hara's turn to smile. "I haven't heard that expression since I was a little boy," he said. "It's not one I'd expect you to use, somehow."

Kimura frowned. His retired diplomat father invariably used the old-fashioned euphemism for dying and he thought it had a certain elegance. "Stick around, Hara," he said rather stiffly, straightening himself in the chair and checking that the knot of his necktie was still nestling snugly at his collar. "I'm full of surprises."

Then he coughed in a businesslike way, like a chairman about to open a meeting. "What I was about to say was that the prosecutor might well feel that the slightly delayed-action murder of one prominent Japanese businessman, the much more efficient killing of one British fashion designer and the infliction of fairly serious injuries on a British journalist within a radius of a hundred metres from this office in the space of a few days might call for some special investigative effort on the part of the Hyogo prefectural police force. And that he might wish to be kept informed about progress, if any."

"Quite. Sarcasm does not become you, Inspector."

The remark took Kimura aback and he hauled himself to his feet before replying. "What's got into you all of a sudden, Hara? You're looking altogether too pleased with yourself for my liking." The tension mounted as the two men stared at each other, but not for long.

Eventually Hara smiled again, flapped a hand at Kimura in a comical little gesture and sank into the visitor's chair. "Sit down again, do," he said. "I enjoy working with you, you know. Don't you think it's time we both relaxed?"

Kimura sat down with evident reluctance, still wary.

"You're quite a bit senior to me in the grade. You really don't have to prove it," Hara went on. "Quite apart from that, I'm the new boy here in Kobe. I know how much the superintendent depends on you and Ninja Noguchi. Can I persuade you that I'm not jealous? Not of that, anyway. I envy you, certainly. I've watched the way you handle the foreigners, and I know I couldn't match it in a thousand years."

173

"Ah, but then you weren't born in Chicago," Kimura said, immediately mollified by Hara's unexpected overtures. "On the other hand I'm no intellectual, I know that quite well. We've needed somebody like you on the team for a long time."

He thought he probably meant it, having begun to realise that the donnish, pedantic manner which had so irritated him about Hara from the outset could be accounted for just as easily in terms of shyness as of a supercilious air of superiority. He grinned again, this time with straightforward good humour. "Anyhow, look at your advantages. Coming after old Sakamoto, you had to be an improvement. All right, no more fencing, then. It's agreed we're on the same side. So you can come clean. You've just been talking to Kuniko Doi, haven't you? So what *are* you looking pleased with yourself about?"

Hara nodded. "Yes. I had three-quarters of an hour with her this morning. She came early specially, at nine-thirty. A strange woman. Shrewd and businesslike, but with a very sentimental streak in her character, in my opinion. She is also an accomplished actress. When we were on our own together in her dressing-room she was sensible, straightforward, unaffected. Then the English girl burst in on us. Vanessa Radley. It was fascinating to see the way Doi-san instantly switched on her television personality the moment she saw her, literally in mid-sentence while she was still talking to me."

"Not surprising. Vanessa Radley's a very attractive girl. There might even be something between them. Not that I can see what the English girl would be likely to get out of going to bed with Kuniko Doi," Kimura added pensively. "She's hardly likely to aspire to a career in Japanese show-business, and Doi's old enough to be her mother anyway."

"True, but she has a remarkable personality, and she is rich and famous. That combination generally results in sexual success for men, whatever their age. Why not for women?"

Kimura gazed at his colleague through narrowed eyes. "I

174

do believe you fancy her yourself, Hara. I wish you lots of luck. What did the English rose want, anyway?"

"I don't know. They spoke English, of course, but I suppose I ought to have been able to grasp a general idea of what they said. The girl seems to have a very strange accent, though. She apologised for interrupting us – that much was obvious. Then she chattered away for a minute or two and I couldn't understand a word. Kuniko Doi got up, went over to the door and put her arm round her and murmured something. It looked odd – the English girl towered over her. Anyway, Miss Radley looked a bit dubious, but took herself off. All Doi-san said after she'd gone was 'What a sweet child!' I didn't press her, but you might bear it in mind if you're talking to the girl later. I was more interested in getting back to the subject of her relationship with Masako Yasuda, and had to keep an eye on the time. Doi-san still had to change and get ready for the eleven o'clock show." He paused to look at his watch. "Which should be starting about now."

"So? What did you find out?" Kimura demanded impatiently. "I haven't got all that long myself. I'm due to talk to Marian Norton again at eleven-twenty and Terry Phipps at noon."

Hara nodded. "I know. Do try to fit in a word with Vanessa Radley if you can, though. Very well, I'll try to be brief. It is of course most unusual for a television personality of Kuniko Doi's status to take on a job like this – to do as many as ten shows over a period of four days, I mean. A guest appearance at the gala preview for a huge fee perhaps, with plenty of publicity. But they really don't need a big name for the regular shows. They could easily hire somebody much less expensive to do the commentaries from behind the scenes. So I asked her frankly why she was prepared to give up so much of her time to Mode International. I've already told you that she was completely matter-of-fact with me while we were alone. She was also very much on guard, though. Choosing her words rather carefully, I thought. She answered me by

175

explaining that it isn't by any means a waste of her time, and that it isn't interfering with her regular interview shows on television. In fact she's recorded two here in Kobe, with women involved in Mode International as guests. Kansai Television made a studio available."

Kimura raised his eyebrows with interest. "Did she mention which women?"

"When I asked her, yes. Masako Yasuda, needless to say, on one show, along with Vanessa Radley and Selena Stoke-Lacy. They recorded that one on the morning of the press conference. The day Watanabe was injured. It was broadcast yesterday, she said. The second show was recorded yesterday evening. Her guests were Marian Norton, Barbi Mingus, the Swedish model who speaks such excellent Japanese, and the young woman from the *Kobe Shimbun*. Nakazato-san. It will go out tomorrow."

Hara hastened on, guessing that Kimura probably needed time to assimilate the news of Mie Nakazato's appearance on the Kuniko Doi chat show. "Doi-san then went on to explain that in any case she was an old friend of both Masako Yasuda and Yutaka Watanabe and that when Yasuda-san asked her as a special favour to do the commentaries she was only too pleased to do so. Not only for the sake of the money – which she described as very satisfactory without specifying the amount – but also because she knew the directors of the Wakamatsu company were trying to remove Watanabe and terminate the Yasuda boutique concession. The greater the impact of Mode International, she implied, the stronger her friends' position would be. I don't know how you would assess her personal contribution to its success so far, but Uehara tells me that attendances and publicity have far surpassed their hopes and expectations. He considers Kuniko Doi to have been a great draw."

"And a couple of murders haven't exactly dampened down the general interest, have they?" Kimura was fidgeting and glancing from time to time at the door, obviously not giving his full attention to what Hara was saying.

176

"I agree. Well, I musn't keep you, but you ought to know one thing before you talk to anybody else. I asked Kuniko Doi if she had any idea who might have killed Wesley Wilberforce. Routinely, as we've been doing with everybody. As you know, people have been inclined to say they can't imagine, and then obliquely hint that it more or less has to be Terry Phipps. Well, Kuniko Doi didn't do that. She looked at me very seriously for quite a long time and then said that in her opinion we ought to investigate Jean-Claud Villon's alibi. She added that it would be interesting to know who is named as the principal beneficiary of Wilberforce's will."

Kimura sucked in air through his teeth in that most Japanese expression of doubtful hesitation; one which he affected to despise when others indulged in it. There was no longer any doubt about his interest in what Hara had to say. "Villon. That *would* be a surprise, I must say," he muttered, then sat up straight. "The chief's ahead of her on the other front. Who benefits financially from Wilberforce's death, I mean. It was one of the first things he asked me to raise with the British Consulate-General. I expect we'll have the answer before long."

Hara disengaged his bulky body from the easy-chair and loomed over his colleague. "Good. You'll talk to Villon again as soon as possible, I take it. I haven't yet mentioned the most important thing Kuniko Doi said. It was that Vanessa Radley told her that Wilberforce always did like to dress up in women's clothes. Then her actual words were 'So I suppose if he had to die he would have preferred it that way.' " The owlish, academic expression which had been absent from Hara's face during the greater part of their conversation was back in position. "It was clear to me that Doi-san knows how Wilberforce died."

Hara's last few words were almost drowned by the ringing of the telephone on the desk, but although Kimura glared down distractedly at the instrument he had no need to ask Hara to repeat them. He snatched up the receiver and barked into it exasperatedly.

"*Hai! Nan des'ka?* Oh. Sorry, chief, I didn't know it was

177

you. No, I do realise that, and normally I . . .yes, I'll bear it in mind. It's just that I was in conference with Hara here. No, I haven't seen her this morning, I haven't been in the main dressing-room yet. One moment, I'll ask Hara."

Kimura put his hand over the mouthpiece. "Have you seen Junko-san today? She was supposed to ring the boss."

Hara shook his head.

"Are you there, sir? No, he hasn't been in there either. Yes, of course one of us will. I see. . . right. Understood. Would you give me the number, please? Right, got it. Yes, of course. Right away."

Kimura replaced the receiver with exaggerated delicacy and pulled a face. "You'd think he'd have more important things on his mind than my telephone manner, wouldn't you? Will you go up, or shall I? No need to talk to her, he says. Just confirm that she's at work as usual and call him back at the district prosecutor's office to let him know. I can't see why he's in such a hurry."

Hara was already half out of the door. "I'll go," he said. "She's my assistant, after all." He was away for less than five minutes, while Kimura fumed to himself about Otani's incorrigible habit of setting up private ploys of his own during an investigation, and with much less justice about the fact that Mie Nakazato had not told him she was to be one of Kuniko Doi's television guests. He simmered down at once when Hara slipped back into the room and closed the door quietly, concern in his face.

"She's not there," he said. "The show's on, and the supervisor's frantically busy. She's also rather worried. Nobody's seen Junko-san this morning, but when they first realised she hadn't turned up somebody noticed her coat and handbag hanging up. The interviews will have to wait, Kimura. We're going to have to search the building."

Kimura slowly picked up the phone again and pushed the buttons to call Otani back. Then he handed the receiver to Hara.

"You tell him," he said quietly. "She's your assistant, after all."

Chapter XXIII

The spotlights and laser beams cavorted as the music surged to its final climax, transforming the lushly romantic main salon of the Tamahimeden wedding hall into a cave of ultramodern, prancing high-technology demons. For, exhausted though they were, the models were professionals directed by a choreographer with a touch of genius. The last show on the last day of Mode International called for that little something extra and the ensemble delivered it, feeding on the excitement and delight of the audience who roared and cheered their approval as the stage gradually filled and the beautiful bodies in their fantasy finery arched and swayed into the final tableau.

Arms folded, Otani watched quietly from a standing position just inside the door, wondering if he had made the right decisions. He felt strangely detached, contemplating quite clear-headedly the possibility that he could be mistaken. Although he took a proper pride in his work and authority sat easily upon him, Otani was not a vain man. He knew very well that a good many of the criminal investigations he had directed had petered out inconclusively; that he had often enough bent the rules, or failed to see something that was staring him in the face.

Above all he knew that he was often unfair to the immediate subordinates on whose loyalty and efficiency he depended. Was there really any good reason why he had not taken Kimura and Hara fully into his confidence during the conference which had ended ten minutes earlier in the long-suffering manager's office, or was he simply enjoying being mysterious with them? Their confusion and anxiety was understandable enough. After his telephone call in the morning they had made a discreet but comprehensive search of the entire building. They had found no trace of Junko Migishima, and although on receiving their further report Otani had assured them that her disappearance was in no sense their responsibility it must have distracted them hopelessly from their interviewing duties.

Otani sighed and shook his head as he unfolded his arms and prepared to slip out into the corridor. It was obvious even to his ignorant eye that the show was almost over. The tableau was complete, the arms of the young people on the stage and catwalk reaching out in the classic show-business gesture compounded of proud arrogance, submission, appeal, love and abandonment as Kuniko Doi rose from her throne and shimmered forward, raising her own heavily jewelled hand to still the applause into an expectant silence as the last tendrils of music drifted away. Otani timed his exit perfectly, closing the door behind him as he heard the mistress of ceremonies begin to speak. Kimura had warned him there would be speeches, and Otani was sure he could put the time to good use in running through his own tactics again in his mind.

"Superintendent Otani does not speak English," Kimura said in that language to the people on his left. "So he has asked me to translate for you, sentence by sentence. You have no objection to English, M. Villon?" The Frenchman shrugged.

180

Kimura waited, but Jean-Claud Villon said nothing and his expression was unreadable, so Kimura shrugged in turn and looked at the others. Barbi Mingus and Vanessa Radley were wearing jeans and sweatshirts but had not yet removed their stage make-up and looked exotic and unreal as they lolled exhausted on an overstuffed sofa covered in burgundy velvet.

Nearby, Marian Norton sat utterly still, the huge eyes sunken in her pallid face fixed impassively on Kimura. By contrast Villon looked relaxed, slumped with one arm draped casually over the back of the easy chair to which Kimura had steered him, the boldly chalk-striped double-breasted jacket of his pre-war Hollywood gangster-style suit hanging open to reveal part of his red braces.

Terry Phipps sat primly upright in his own chair, which he had pulled no more than a few inches away from Villon's but with the effect of signalling his dissociation from the proceedings. Kimura was worried about Phipps, who not only looked pale and drawn but whose knees twitched up and down rhythmically while from time to time he brushed at a seemingly uncontrollable muscular tic in his left cheek.

They were in one of the smaller Tamahimeden salons, normally used for the popular low-budget wedding receptions involving no more than forty persons in all. It was nevertheless a sizeable, lavishly-furnished room, with a touch of cloying sweetness lingering in its atmosphere as though marking the passage of the powdered, perfumed bodies of the hundreds of brides who had flowered there briefly since it was first used. The decor was vaguely Regency, involving wall-covering with broad vertical crimson stripes on a creamy ground, and curtains hung in swathes against false windows behind which were cunningly illuminated enlargements of photographs of the formal gardens of some stately European residence.

Kimura glanced across to where Hara was presiding over the Japanese-speakers. Masako Yasuda was haggardly bony in silk of a rich blue, while Kuniko Doi was whispering to her, still wearing the glittering trouser-suit in which she had

181

appeared on stage. Hiroshi Uehara sat a little apart, occasionally taking a fine linen handkerchief from his sleeve and dabbing delicately at his forehead with it.

Kimura had long ceased to admire or to be envious of the younger man's dress sense. He was much too tired. Furthermore he was depressed, his head ached, and he greatly doubted Otani's wisdom in insisting that the organisers and the overseas visitors participating in Mode International should be assembled immediately after the end of the final show so that he could address them all together.

It had not been easy for Kimura to round up the ones for whom he was responsible, with the exception of the two models who in any case had to be on the premises until the very end. The original Mode International plan had envisaged a grand celebration party following the finale, but the death first of Wesley Wilberforce and then of Yutaka Watanabe had ruled out anything of the kind. It now seemed that people wanted only to get away as soon as possible, and when Kimura spoke to them both Marian Norton and Jean-Claud Villon had made endless difficulties about staying at the Tamahimeden for the last show at all, let alone remaining afterwards.

So far as Terry Phipps was concerned it was a question of Kimura's arranging for his assistant Migishima to fetch him from the hotel room in which he had effectively re-imprisoned himself since returning there from police headquarters. Phipps had been made aware that he would be prevented from leaving Japan until police enquiries were complete; he had fallen into a trance-like listlessness which Kimura had failed to break through during several frustrating interviews, and which persisted to the extent that he gazed vacantly at those who greeted him warily when Kimura ushered him into the room and made no response even to Vanessa who alone showed warmth towards him, running over and kissing him on the cheek.

Having fulfilled his instructions and delivered Terry Phipps, Migishima himself stood with massive stolidity in one corner of the room. Kimura took it particularly hard that Otani had given specific orders that Junko's husband was to be present. While being briefed over the phone to bring the Englishman to the Tamahimeden Migishima had glumly confirmed that his wife had left their flat before he woke up and that he knew of no reason why she should not have presented herself for work in the dressing-room as usual. It was small wonder the poor fellow looked tense and miserable, Kimura reflected. It was intolerable of Otani to have forbidden him in advance to give the young man the rest of the day off to do whatever he could to track his missing wife down.

" 'Ere, woss appnin, then?" Kimura looked at Vanessa, whose aristocratic features were expressive of boredom, discontent and impatience in equal measure. "Where's iss bloke of yours? Avin a wank or what?" The ugly whine of her voice seemed to echo through the room, and whether or not anyone except possibly the distraught Terry Phipps had the least idea what she was saying, all heads turned in her direction. Kimura cleared his throat and looked round, realising that although his little flock knew no Japanese, everybody in the room at least understood English.

"I'm truly sorry to keep you all waiting, ladies and gentlemen," he said. "The Superintendent is a few minutes later than he said he would be, but I'm sure he'll be here any minute. If you'll just remain here with my colleague Inspector Hara for a moment I'll go and –" Kimura broke off and jumped to his feet as the door was flung open and a grim-faced Otani walked in, took up a position midway between him and Hara who had also risen, and nodded curtly to each of the two inspectors in turn. At some stage during the day he had changed into uniform, and after slowly and deliberately surveying every other person in the room he removed his cap with its braided peak, tucked it under one arm and bowed with cold formality.

"My name is Otani. Commander of the Hyogo prefectural police force. I am sorry to have kept you waiting and sorry

183

indeed that it was necessary to require your presence at this meeting at all." He stood rigidly to attention while Kimura translated, and then relaxed his stance, took a few paces to one side and laid his hat on a side-table before continuing in a more conversational tone, his hands behind his back.

"The meeting was necessary because now that the series of fashion shows known as Mode International has come to an end you will all be hoping and expecting to leave Kobe, many of you indeed to leave Japan." All eyes were upon the stocky, swarthy man, compact in his neat blue uniform, and once more he allowed his gaze to linger for a second or so on each face in turn.

"Yes. I am aware that you all probably have business, professional or personal commitments elsewhere. I shall therefore try to be concise, but must warn you that it will inevitably take some time for me to explain to those of you who were not responsible for them why the success of Mode International has been marred by a sequence of tragic occurrences. In due course you will learn what action my officers and I have taken, the progress of our investigations and the implications of our findings for each of you personally. Please sit down, Inspector Hara. And you, Inspector Kimura."

This time as Kimura interpreted Otani strolled to the other end of the room and murmured to Migishima, who also after some hesitation found himself a chair and perched himself uncomfortably on the edge of the seat.

"You are all aware that during the course of the party given here immediately after the press conference Mr Yutaka Watanabe sustained serious head injuries when a massive chandelier fell on him. Mr Watanabe died, as a consequence of those injuries, the day before yesterday. During the course of the gala preview performance the body of Mr Wesley Wilberforce was discovered in one of the small changing-rooms. The circumstances were such that it was clear that he had been murdered. Two evenings ago Miss Selena Stoke-Lacy, a British fashion writer, was seriously hurt in a traffic

184

accident. Finally, a young lady employed here as what is I understand called an assistant dresser apparently arrived for work this morning but went missing shortly thereafter. It was established during the course of the morning that she was nowhere on the premises. In the light of everything else that has been happening this week, it is hardly surprising that the disappearance of this young woman has given rise to much anxiety. Two people killed, one badly injured, and one missing. The question must inevitably be asked: are these events linked in any way?"

Otani had told himself over and over again to be careful about catching any particular person's eye for too long, but when it came to the point he found it extremely difficult to prevent himself from doing so. He was also briefly, insanely seized with a desire to giggle as it occurred to him that the set-piece situation he had himself contrived was ludicrously similar to those in which Nero Wolfe and other fictional sleuths of the golden-age murder mysteries assembled and confronted their principal suspects, the murderer among them. Otani hastily suppressed the irrational impulse to laugh as he waited for Kimura to finish interpreting his last remarks. There was nothing funny about the task still before him, and the circumstances were very different from those of the session with Uehara alone, when he had been able to sit back unobtrusively and study the man's face while Hara and Kimura between them did all the hard work. Now he had to depend on them to watch reactions, while he could do no more than give voice to his carefully marshalled thoughts, without the benefit of reference to the notes tucked away in his breast pocket.

"The answer to that question is yes," he continued, addressing the air just above the heads of his listeners. "Of course these events are linked, just as the lives – and deaths – of the people involved in them are linked. The origins of this story lie a good many years in the past, when the House of Yasuda was first established. Masako Yasuda had been the mistress of Yutaka Watanabe for a couple of years by then."

Now he could glare directly at her, daring her to interrupt him. In fact she tensed and seemed momentarily to be about to do so, but Kuniko Doi placed a cautionary hand on her arm and she remained silent, her eyes glittering.

"I am not insulting you. Your former relationship with Watanabe is a matter of common knowledge, Madame Yasuda," he said. "Moreover Watanabe's widow is in Kobe at present, and has made a full statement to us about her late husband's extra-marital activities. Those – such as his affair with you – which entailed substantial or continuing financial commitments, anyway. Mrs Watanabe is, as you well know, a woman of strong character who has always made it her business to avail herself of expert legal advice so as to protect her own interests. She has also from time to time over the years employed private investigators who have provided her with a considerable mass of documented evidence of Watanabe's irregular and often illegal activities in various contexts which I do not need to describe in detail here. You knew about a good many of those activities, and you put that knowledge to practical use when Watanabe became bored with your sexual services and attempted to discard you as he had discarded other women before you; an attempt you had realistically foreseen and made preparations to turn to your advantage. Indeed, you probably welcomed his loss of interest in you, for you had a great deal to occupy you at that time."

During the frequent pauses while Kimura translated for him, Otani's eyes seldom left Masako Yasuda's mask-like face, but he also observed the conflicting reactions which seemed to fight for supremacy in Uehara's expression as the story unfolded.

"Watanabe was not an ungenerous man, and had already given you considerable financial and other help in securing Tokyo premises and setting up your own fashion house. You had originality and flair, and deserved your early success at a time when Japanese fashion was just beginning to attract international attention. You were in a hurry, though, and

186

needed more from Watanabe. You therefore threatened to expose and ruin him unless he paid your price. This was the exclusive contract for Yasuda boutiques in the Wakamatsu department store chain of which he was the president."

Otani paused once more and nodded to Kimura, transferring his gaze to the group of foreigners. Even Terry Phipps stopped fidgetting and stared back as Kimura summarised what he had said. "Sentence by sentence from now on, please, Inspector," Otani said when he had finished.

"The Yasuda boutiques did well, but within a very few years Masako Yasuda wanted international links. First you, Miss Norton, eased her path in America and became a close personal friend. You, Mr Villon, did the same in France, and comparatively recently Wesley Wilberforce, who had known Madame Yasuda for many years, offered similar help in England. As you are well aware, Mr Phipps. In return Madame Yasuda promised to arrange through Watanabe for your products to be promoted in the prestigious Wakamatsu department-store chain, and indeed succeeded in doing so in the first two cases. Arrangements on behalf of Wesley Wilberforce hung fire, mainly because Mr Uehara here was unenthusiastic about his products and by then had achieved a good deal of influence in the House of Yasuda. Nevertheless everything seemed to be going along quite satisfactorily until about a year ago. Then two things happened. The first was that Watanabe's relationship with his fellow Wakamatsu directors – always somewhat stormy – deteriorated sharply and it became obvious that his position was becoming very precarious. The second disturbing factor was the meteoric rise to international fame of Tsutomu Kubota and his determination to break up your cosy little club."

Otani permitted himself the merest suggestion of a smile as several of his audience looked around and it appeared to dawn on them that Kubota was not among those present. "No, Mr Kubota is not here. I expect him to arrive shortly, though. In fact. . ." He looked at his watch, then turned towards Migishima and raised his voice slightly. "If you would be so kind, officer?" Migishima jumped to his feet at once and went out of the door, leaving it open behind him. The silence was profound, until it was broken by the sound of voices in the corridor. Then Tsutomu Kubota walked in, followed by Junko Migishima and Ninja Noguchi, with Junko's husband bringing up the rear.

Terry Phipps half-rose in his seat, and then launched himself bodily at Kubota. "So it *was* you, you bastard!" he screamed.

Chapter XXIV

Tough and seasoned though they both were, it took the combined efforts of both Noguchi and Migishima to seize and hold the frantically struggling man back from Kubota, who had backed away in the face of the onslaught. Kimura was on his feet but he too had been taken by surprise and it was not until Otani snapped at him that he pulled himself together, crossed swiftly to where Phipps had been pinioned by the arms and administered a stinging slap to the face which momentarily stilled the Englishman.

"Tell him he's wrong, Kimura. Tell him Kubota had nothing to do with Wilberforce's death. And tell him that we know he didn't, either." Kimura did his best. At first it was impossible to judge whether or not he was getting through to Phipps, but after the third or fourth repetition Phipps's staring eyes seemed to come into focus at last, and a little later all the fight went out of him. He slumped between his hefty captors and would have fallen had Migishima not continued to support him and eased him back to his chair.

Otani looked swiftly round at all the others, making it clear that he was speaking for their benefit as well as for that of Terry Phipps. "Tell Mr Phipps that he has my profound sympathy in his distress, and that I can well imagine what an ordeal it has been for him to have to endure not only his grief over the death of his friend but also the realisation that some of the people in this room have suspected him of having been responsible for it. I must ask you all to bear with me for a little longer, because now that Mr Kubota has joined us – along with my colleagues Inspector Noguchi and Woman Senior Detective Migishima – the time has come for an explanation of the events of the recent past. You look surprised, Mr Uehara. So do you, Miss Norton. In fact you all do. Except Mr Kubota, who has already spent rather more time in Mrs Migishima's company today than he expected to. Be patient. What I have to say will not take much longer."

He nodded towards the little group still near the door and Migishima and Junko moved away, leaving Noguchi massively in position barring the exit. Junko placed herself beside the sofa on which Vanessa Radley and Barbi Mingus were both now sitting bolt upright while her husband led Kubota to the group beside Hara and stood behind him when he sat down.

While this was happening Otani drew Kimura to one side and spoke to him rapidly in an undertone. "I know what you must be thinking, Kimura-kun. Forgive me. I'll explain later, but this really was the only way I could think of to cope with the situation."

Without waiting to study Kimura's reaction, he turned back to the others. "Kubota's activities posed a threat to the interests of the House of Yasuda. Watanabe's mounting difficulties with his fellow-directors posed an even greater one. If he were to be dismissed in disgrace Masako Yasuda would undoubtedly forfeit her immensely lucrative privileges, and so, very possibly, might her foreign associates. On the other hand, were Watanabe to die in office the Wakamatsu directors would almost certainly wish to avoid a

190

scandal and subsequent damage to the firm's reputation, which would itself have financial consequences. Masako Yasuda therefore hurriedly set about making certain arrangements. From having been no more than a vague idea, Mode International assumed concrete form. Hiroshi Uehara was very cleverly persuaded that the arrangements he made developed logically and naturally rather than having been conceived in detail from the outset by his employer. She brought the people she wanted to the place she wanted them in and as quickly as she reasonably could. While waiting for this to happen she somehow pressurised Watanabe to renew her Wakamatsu contract, confident that it would not in fact be repudiated by the other directors because she was still close enough to her former lover to know when his dismissal from the board would be imminent, and intended to make sure that he died before that happened – as indeed he did. The Tokyo police are currently following up some interesting suggestions made to us in that connection by Mrs Watanabe."

Otani wheeled round and spoke again directly to Masako Yasuda who stared back at him, the last traces of colour drained from her face. Hara shifted a mere inch or so nearer to her but then froze as Otani directed a thunderous look at him. "You intimidated your own company, Madame Yasuda, with the willing but amateurish assistance of your unscrupulous hireling Kinjo. No, there's no point in looking round, he isn't here. You knew there would be trouble here this week, because you intended to arrange it; so you set up an imaginary guilty party in advance. You probably also had the idea that a substantial sum of money in a Swiss bank account might be useful to fall back on if something went wrong, and no doubt originally planned to authorise Mr Uehara to pay it. But things did go wrong. Why you imagined that Kinjo was competent to rig up a booby trap like that, which would have taxed the ingenuity of an expert, we find it hard to understand. Perhaps you didn't care who happened to be underneath it when it fell, never supposing that it might kill anybody. Perhaps you intended it merely as a showy piece of phony evidence that the fictitious extortioners meant business, so that Tsutomu Kubota's subsequent death could be attributed to them. It's unimportant now. The fact is that the chandelier fell on Watanabe's head. That in itself did not distress you greatly, except perhaps to the extent that you would have preferred him to have died at once, rather than later."

Masako Yasuda remained rigidly tense, but Otani noted that not only had Kuniko Doi removed her hand from her friend's arm but also edged away and was staring at her in undisguised horror.

"Unfortunately for you, Mr Kubota already had his suspicions about this whole enterprise, remembered that you had summoned him to your side minutes before the incident and surmised that he might have been the intended victim. He went to see Watanabe in hospital and had an interesting talk with him. He then discussed the matter not only with his former wife Miss Selena Stoke-Lacy, with whom he remains on amicable terms, but also with Wesley Wilberforce, the man you first met when you were a young woman in Paris, with whom you fell in love at that time and who rejected you for reasons you could not at the time understand. Mr Wilberforce was an honourable man who was greatly shocked by what Mr Kubota suggested, and urged him to inform the police. Mr Kubota declined to do so at that stage, whereupon Mr Wilberforce resolved to do so himself. He was misguided enough to discuss his intention with another person, without however revealing that Mr Kubota had been the source of the information which so disturbed him."

Otani suddenly felt very tired, and was conscious of a powerful urge to have the guilty taken away without more ado, but then caught sight of the expression on Terry Phipps's face and knew he had to go on. "Tragedy might have been avoided if only he had confided in Mr Phipps, but the two were indulging in one of their habitual meaningless childish quarrels, which also unfortunately meant that Mr Wilberforce was alone for long enough for his killer to strangle him and leave his body in circumstances suggesting that his assailant had been a homosexual: obviously to throw suspicion on Mr Phipps himself. The body was discovered . . . accidentally. Mrs Migishima – who has been keeping these premises and some of you under observation all week – was the first police officer on the scene."

He switched his gaze to Kimura. "Translate this next part with special care, Inspector, if you please," he said, and then wheeled to face Marian Norton, whose face was as white and strained as Masako Yasuda's.

"So, Miss Norton, I come to you. For it was you who killed Wesley Wilberforce in order to protect your old and dear friend Masako Yasuda, counting on her to deal with Mr Kubota – who constitutes a direct threat to your business in New York also – according to her original intention as confided to you. It was a mistake to put the torn wrapper from the *obishime* cord you used to strangle Wilberforce in Kinjo's pocket in an attempt to implicate him, by the way. Yes, it was found, and when confronted with it this afternoon Kinjo – who is under arrest, by the way – sensibly decided that there were limits to his loyalty and told us a great many interesting things. He is a shabby little crook but no murderer."

Otani's voice became quieter and less accusing, taking on a note almost of puzzlement. "You are as calculating and ruthless as your friend, and if anything even more evil. It was an act of pure intellectual sadism to dress Wilberforce's body as you did, knowing of Masako Yasuda's former frustrated love for him. And then you coolly decided that, to be on the safe side, Miss Stoke-Lacy needed to be silenced also. The fact that she and Kubota had been married was well known to you all, of course. It took us in the police a little longer to come by the information. You – or more probably Madame Yasuda, whose car is undergoing expert examination at this moment – bungled your attempt to kill the lady, who is sufficiently recovered to give her own testimony. The death of Mr Wilberforce obviously both horrified and alarmed Mr Kubota, and the attack on his former wife was enough to

193

prompt him to confide to some extent in my colleague Inspector Noguchi over there, who first became acquainted with him many years ago. It is just as well. Miss Norton, you were terrified yesterday when Mrs Migishima allowed you to infer that she was in posession of crucial information about Wilberforce's murder. She was indeed, but not of the kind you supposed. Mrs Migishima expected you to be lying in wait for her early this morning. Mr Kubota's arrival on the scene just as you were about to try to kill her was, of course, planned. He did not in fact save Mrs Migishima's life: she is very well equipped to take care of herself. It did, however, throw you off balance and leave you guessing when she went off so willingly with him."

Kimura was having to work hard. Otani did not in fact stop after every sentence to give him time to interpret, and he screwed up his eyes from time to time as he tried to render quite lengthy chunks of the calm, almost reflective exposition accurately into English. He did not therefore react as quickly as Junko when Vanessa Radley gave a stifled, choking scream and flung herself at Marian Norton, fingers and nails aimed at her face.

"Save the rest until we take her statement, Kimura-kun," Otani advised as he surveyed the mêlée and Hara raised Masako Yasuda to her feet, firmly grasping her by the upper arm. "We can clear things up with the others here a lot more quickly when they're both out of the way."

He turned his back and distanced himself by a few paces from the confusion. The dresses on their rails looked cheap and tawdry to him, like Masako Yasuda's furtive, consuming greed and the poisonous bud of misunderstanding which had so disgustingly flowered in the actions of the American. Otani wearily rubbed his eyes, feeling soiled by the appropriate banality of his own performance.

Chapter XXV

It was a beautiful day for the Grand All-Kansai Bonsai Festival; and Hanae knew that it was that which probably tipped the scale and persuaded her husband to go at all, let alone face up to his responsibilities as President of the Rokko District Bonsai Club. She had seldom before seen him looking so tired and drawn as he had been on finally arriving home late in the evening after supervising the arrest of Masako Yasuda and Marian Norton, and he had slept heavily but restlessly that night and left early for his office again in the morning. By evening he was looking a little better and had even volunteered a very brief account of his conclusions about the case, now supported by a series of amendments to the statements previously made by most of those principally involved. The detailed questioning of Masako Yasuda and Marian Norton was to be handled at more leisure. Otani already knew that both would have high-powered legal advice, and Kimura in particular would have all his work cut out to handle the American Consulate-General.

That morning Otani had merely groaned unintelligibly when Hanae brought him a cup of green tea, reminded him that it was Saturday and urged him to be up and doing. The next couple of hours had been very heavy going for her, but now in the early afternoon she looked round and sniffed the air appreciatively, delighted to see how many people in cheerful clothes were milling about the brave display of row upon row of tiny trees, each in its carefully selected and often very valuable ceramic bowl, arranged on tiers of shelving in the exhibition area of the park on fashionable, man-made Port Island in Kobe Harbour.

It was one of those exhilarating days which can make early winter in western Japan the most perfect season in the world. Pressure was high, the sun sparkled down from a cloudless, arching sky of palest blue, and Hanae knew that the grumpy husband who had unwillingly got himself dressed, and eventually consented with an ill grace to be towed down to the Portliner railcar terminus at Sannomiya, was now secretly in a state of high delight. The lovely weather and Hanae's reminder that he would probably meet his new friends from Accrington again helped, the Chinese lunch including his favourite prawn with ginger sweetened him further, and the discovery, when they arrived at the display area, that Otani's own miniature maple had been awarded a Silver Prize did the rest.

He pretended to be blasé about it, but accepted the congratulations of his Vice-President and the assembled committee members with what to Hanae was obvious glee, and made no objection at all when their neighbour Mr Sugimoto's pretty teenage daughter insisted on pinning to his lapel an enormous artificial chrysanthemum with streamers on which were written his name and superior status in the world of organised bonsai. Having contentedly stood by for several minutes as Otani chatted with increasing geniality to his little band of acolytes, and exchanged a word or two herself with Mrs Sugimoto, Hanae left them to it and drifted over towards the chrysanthemum display which constituted the other half of the exhibition.

"I'm glad you talked him into coming, Mrs Otani. Good afternoon." She recognised the voice at her shoulder immediately and turned round with a dazzling smile.

"Why, Mr Kimura, how very nice to see you here! Isn't it a lovely day!" The smile faded as Hanae took in the dark patches under Kimura's eyes, which in any case seemed to lack their customary sparkle. Even the knot of his necktie was slightly askew, producing an effect which would have been unnoticeable in the overwhelming majority of men but was shocking and disturbing where Kimura was concerned.

"Yes, lovely," he agreed. "Is it really only a few days since we met at the Japan-British Society reception?"

Hanae nodded. "It seems a lot longer to me too. From what little my husband has mentioned, I can imagine how exhausting all this must have been for you."

Kimura made a valiant effort to shake off his lethargy and summon up the reserves of gallantry which normally dictated his manner when in the company of any woman, let alone one as handsome as Hanae Otani. "All in the day's work for us, Ma'am. But you had a dreadful experience. Deeply distressing."

They watched in silence as a small girl wandered by, her eyes raised to her bright pink, helium balloon. "She ought to have the string tied round her wrist," Hanae said pensively, fighting hard to suppress the image of the ghastly face of Wesley Wilberforce turned towards her. "She'll soon lose it otherwise."

"I don't think they really mind, you know. It must be rather nice to watch them soar higher and higher and imagine they're on the way to the moon. It's the prize-giving ceremony soon, I think. Congratulations on the Superintendent's Silver Prize, by the way. Had you realised who will be presenting it to him?"

Hanae looked again into the tired eyes. "No. Who?"

"Kuniko Doi. I didn't know myself until I saw it on the local news on TV this morning. The city government did well to get her. She's a big crowd-puller. Ironic, though, isn't it? Are you going to go over and watch?"

Hanae shook her head. "I don't think so, thank you. I'll stay here and enjoy the chrysanthemums and let my husband tell me about it later. Oh, look! Isn't that Miss Doi just arriving? Look, over there."

Kimura followed her glance. "Yes, that's her. . ." he began, and then stood very still.

Hanae felt that Kuniko Doi's public image was so well established that she might be a little daring. "I see she has one of her famous girl-friends with her," she said. "I wonder who it is?"

"I know her, actually," Kimura replied in a peculiar voice after what seemed a long time. "She's a reporter on the *Kobe Shimbun*."

"Well, back to Brother Yamanaka and Divine Possession on Monday," Junko said lazily. She and her husband were in bed, and had been dozing after making love. "All the same, the job at the Tamahimeden turned out to be more interesting than I'd expected."

"Yes. Nevertheless, I still think it was unfair of the superintendent to ask you to do anything so risky." Migishima relapsed into silence and then abruptly raised himself on one elbow and looked down at her suspiciously. "What did he mean, by the way? About you 'going off so willingly' with Kubota? What actually happened that morning?"

"Oh, nothing," Junko said, and then gave a creamy little laugh. "Just a little scene we staged to give the American woman the wrong idea. Nothing for you to worry your head over." Then she pulled him back down on to her warm body and slid her hands over his back. "Come on, we don't have to get up yet."

It was true, then, hard as it was for him to accept. Well, Mie had hinted as much on the last occasion he had seen her, and their conversation on the telephone the previous evening ought to have left him in no doubt. It was just as well that Mrs

Otani had decided to stay with the chrysanthemums. Kimura edged nearer to the crowd of autograph-hunters besieging Kuniko Doi and studied the expression on Mie's face as she gazed at the woman whose arm she was clutching. He needed no further confirmation, and hastily turned away as, to his embarrassment and astonishment, he felt a prickling behind his eyes and his vision became blurred. He supposed he must have been more than a little in love with the girl after all, and now she was gone. Very probably because he had bungled things so hopelessly on the one occasion she had been ready and willing, too. Well, it served him right, and it was ridiculous for a man of his age and experience to react so childishly. Kimura blew his nose noisily and marched off in the direction of the refreshment kiosk. A cup of coffee would be the thing, he thought.

"Cheer up, we'll all soon be dead!" cried Sara Byers-Pinkerton merrily, spilling some of her own coffee down her skirt. "Oh, bugger it, never mind, it'll wash. What about a tune on that old fiddle-face of yours, then? You ought to be cock-a-hoop, Mister super-sleuth. What are you doing at this ghastly orgy anyway? Douglas dragged me here. He's into bonsai, would you believe it?"

She crossed her eyes comically and Kimura felt his spirits rising as he smiled and let her babble on, since she clearly expected no reply from him. "They say the forties is the dangerous age, but I never expected to lose his affections to a scruffy little plant, of all things. Hope he catches us together, don't you? I shall encourage him to fear the worst."

"You did that last time," Kimura pointed out when she eventually paused for breath. "It didn't work. How's Selena, by the way? I'm afraid I shall have to ask her to give me a statement fairly soon."

The eyes rounded in Mrs B-P's mobile face and she prodded Kimura quite painfully on the breast-bone. "Much better. Coming back to the house tomorrow. But pining dreadfully for you, you heartless beast. Don't think we didn't see you in that clinch outside our house."

"Oh, I can explain –"

"Explain? I've got eyes in my head. And ears attached, one each side. I've been to see her in hospital, even if you haven't. Heart to heart. Girls together. She fancies you madly, I'll have you know."

"Really?" Kimura felt very much better. "I think you're kidding me."

"I kid you not," Mrs B-P said earnestly. "And the question arises what you're proposing to do about it. Hah! Give you a statement, indeed. Selena will be staying with us for the next three or four weeks to convalesce. I suggest you begin by coming for drinks tomorrow evening. Sixish."

"Really?" Kimura said again. "That's very kind of you. I shall look forward to it."

"And I," Mrs B-P announced, "shall warn Douglas yet again that it's me you're really after."